"Um, Jeremy," I said, "is it definite about our bike hike on Saturday?"

"Yeah, sure. Unless it rains or something. Why do you ask?"

"Oh, no reason. It's just, well, Mary Alice had this brainstorm. She mentioned double-dating, and I said . . ."

"Double-dating? She probably means with her and Don." Jeremy crinkled his nose. "Personally, I consider Mary Alice bad news. But, what the heck, why not? Okay, tell her we'll go."

"Mary Alice didn't mean *you*," I blurted out. "She was talking about Arnold Greene. And me. . . ."

"Excuse me," said Jeremy, in a thick voice. And off he zoomed.

IT'S NEVER EASY

JEAN F. CAPRON

SCHOLASTIC INC.
New York Toronto London Auckland Sydney Tokyo

To Harry

ISBN 0-590-32408-X

12 11 10 9 8 7 6 5 4 3 2 1 9 3 4 5 6 7/8

Printed in the U. S. A. 06

ONE

Sometimes, when things went real blah for me, running downhill all the way (as they often did last spring), I'd stay awake half the night brooding about it. Especially after my dad would start the ball rolling with a crack like, "Buck up, girl! Don't you know the teens are the best years of a person's life?"

As I blurted out to Jeremy one day, "Big deal! Who needs the extra pain?"

Jeremy just looked at me and grinned. He was only too familiar with my blurting mood.

The day that conversation took place, we were hanging around the Arbutus Street baseball lot, waiting for the rest of the team to show up for afternoon practice. Jeremy was getting out the equipment (four scarred, old bats, a catcher's mask, and a six-pack of baseballs), and I was setting out the makeshift slabs we used to mark the bases. I was moving slowly. Barely dragging along. It had been a particularly nothing week for me.

Jeremy trained his big eyes on me. "Maybe you're just overreacting, Red," he said. Then, digging his manager's rulebook from his back pocket, he frowned, as if concentrating on something, and busily penciled something in the margin of a page. After a minute he looked up again. "So what if Mary Alice did make a couple of stupid remarks?" he shot at me. "Why do you allow that pain in the neck to get to you?"

I didn't think he'd even heard my under-the-breath muttering about Mary Alice Martinson. She and I had suffered through an off-again, on-again friendship for years. Things between us would go along pretty smoothly, then she'd start to meddle, offer heavy-handed suggestions, and tell me how to run my life. I liked my life just the way it was. Why would I want to change it?

As for Jeremy, he always did have this remarkable talent for knowing exactly what was bugging me — even when I couldn't put it into words. At times he was so sharp he scared me. (But then, we just about broke even on that score. I mean, I'd picked up a few vibrations from Jeremy Barnes along the way. Some of which to this day he doesn't realize that I've received. And if I use my head and keep my mouth shut, he never will.)

Part of the reason Jeremy and I had this rapport was that we'd known each other practically since diaper days. He, his older sister, and his parents lived across the street, in the comfortable, old, three-story stucco house the

Barneses had occupied since the year one. And we Shepards (Dad, Mom, my older brother Mike, and I) had been residents of Arbutus Street for as long as I could remember. Jeremy and I had started kindergarten together and worked up to where we were last spring: freshmen at Wilmont High. He was a few months older than I. But since he wasn't very tall and had this round face, melting brown eyes, dark hair that curled when it was damp, and ears that stuck out and turned red easily, he gave the appearance of being somewhat younger than fifteen.

Still, long ears of knowing each other didn't tell the whole story of what Jeremy Barnes and I had going for us. I realized, in a dim way, there was something pretty special about the kid. A sort of inner eagerness. At times it worried me. I would go out of my way to shield Jeremy from anyone or anything that might hurt him.

Little did I dream the day would come when I'd forget all about my urge to shield Jeremy. Or that my dabbling in the big world out there would bring both of us such pain.

But more of that as I go along.

I slapped third base into place and reached for the canvas-covered home plate. "She called me emotionally retarded," I said. Grimly, I guess, because that was how I felt. "Mary Alice figures any fourteen-year-old girl who's still playing infield for the Arbutus Street Gophers and considers herself one of the guys has to have something terribly wrong with her brain." I straightened up and, hugging home plate to my sweat-shirted chest, eyed Jeremy. "Tell me the truth," I said. "Do I strike you as emotionally retarded?"

Jeremy stared somberly at me over the top of his rulebook. Then this tender smile curved his lips. "You? Emotionally retarded?" The smile reached his eyes, doing great things for his homely-nice face. "Never!" And then his gaze shifted. "But one thing I would suggest, Red," he added offhandedly. "Get yourself a new sweat shirt. That one's a little, uh, small."

Before I had a chance to mull over what message (if any) Jeremy was trying to convey, the rest of the Gophers showed up, and we got down to the business of mapping out baseball strategy.

Still, I must admit that it wouldn't have mattered anyway. I mean, last spring I was just not into what the rapidly developing condition under my ratty, old sweat shirt was supposed to be telling me.

I was, however, into several other absorbing projects. At that particular moment, sandlot baseball. The Gophers were considering me for the position of shortstop, and that day our practice was to focus on developing an effective doubleplay. I was agile, quick, and competitive. And I had my heart set on becoming the top shortstop in our sectional league. Jeremy, whose talent was in managing, had assured me I had as good a chance as any of the guys.

Jeremy and I were also into fossil collecting and bike hiking and exploring spooky old houses. The boy-girl thing? Well . . . certainly I didn't consider him a Tarzan, with yours truly playing

Jane. He was just my good old buddy, Jeremy Barnes, and I was . . . me. Red (Jody) Shepard. Only incidentally a girl.

Anyway, the rest of the Gophers huddled around Jeremy, while he worked on who was to occupy which position. "And, of course, Red will play shortstop," he mentioned in passing, assigning Bob Murray to center field.

"What do you mean, 'of course'?" Bob growled, hunching his heavily muscled shoulders. "Last month you had *me* penciled in for shortstop. Now, all of a sudden, *she* . . ." He shook his forefinger at me. Accusing or threatening — I wasn't sure which. But I'd run into that kind of flak before. So I just kept my face still, stood my ground, and let Jeremy do the talking.

Which, believe me, Jeremy could do. It was an education to watch the boy in action. "But, Bob," he started off reasonably, "you know you have a great throwing arm. And the outfield has always been our weak link. I can't think of one other guy better suited to center field than you."

After a few more honeyed words, Bob obediently trotted out to the field. But even Jeremy's skill couldn't entirely wipe the frown from Bob Murray's face. I should have anticipated what was soon to happen.

For a while we fiddled around with double-play techniques, trying this, trying that, getting it down pat. And then we worked on snagging pop flies. Then Dave Lansing popped one, just a little high, in my direction. I hustled back and raised my glove, waiting for the satisfying thump of a caught ball.

I got my thump. Right between the shoulder blades, where Bob Murray, loping toward the infield, caught *me*.

I tried to gather some breath. From a prone position, with the oxygen draining out of me, this wasn't easy. And staring up into Bob's scowling face didn't help.

"That was *my* ball," he sizzled. "Who d'you think you are, hogging the whole field?"

I made it to my knees. "Your ball, my eye," I snapped. "And watch who you're shoving around, Murray!" I plucked his fingers from my sleeve.

Jeremy hollered something from the sidelines, but Bob and I were too busy exchanging glares to listen. Bob's eyes narrowed. "Look at yourself," he croaked. "Hair like a rat's nest, face streaked with dirt . . ." His eyes suddenly changed expression. "And that dinky, little sweat shirt, all torn . . ."

I glanced down, then felt my cheeks go hot. For all practical purposes, my sweat shirt was no longer serving a function.

Bob reached out a hand to help me up. I hesitated, then gave in and accepted it. He watched me work busily at brushing myself off. Then, grinning, he leaned forward. "Tell you something, Red," he confided. "Your best bet would be to run home, change your sweat shirt to something decent, and start acting like a *girl*."

I stiffened. "So who asked you, Murray?"

At which point, Jeremy chose to saunter over. "Good grief, Red," he said, "what a sight! Why don't you run home, change your sweat shirt, and —"

Ordinarily, I don't lose my temper easily. And until that moment, I can't remember ever flaring up at Jeremy. So it shook me as much as it did him when I yelled, "Oh, you shut *up*," burst into tears, and lit on out of there.

As I ran, my ears picked up Jeremy's protests and Bob Murray's drawl: "What did you expect, Barnes? She is a girl. And you know how *they* are."

Funny how a remark can hit home. I mean, until then I'd considered myself . . . you know. Just me. And suddenly I'd been dumped into a category. I was one of *them*. A *girl*.

My mother was in the kitchen, stirring frozen peas into her stew. When she glanced up and saw me her eyes widened. You could almost see the questions hovering in midair. But I hurried on past her and up the stairs.

I told myself I needed to be alone to think everything out. But it occurred to me, as I stretched full length on my bed with only the ticking of an alarm clock to break the silence, that I wasn't doing too well. Aloneness had never been my big thing. Usually I turned to Jeremy.

I closed my eyes, trying to picture myself confiding my jumbled state of emotions to Jeremy. But I was having enough trouble sorting them out for myself.

I'd invested a lot of good years in being one of the guys, one of the Arbutus Street Gophers — mixing it up in our backyard, fighting over a football, hanging around the Barneses' front porch steps on Saturday nights with Jeremy and Bob and Benny Armand, gabbing about this and that, spinning tall tales, teasing, pulling dumb practical jokes. I mean, you just don't trash that kind of pleasure.

But lately there had been moments . . .

Like, at times I would react to ordinary situations in the most puzzling ways. For instance, watching the sun go down or hearing the strains of certain wistful music would slow me to a near trance, make me yearn for . . . for what? I had no idea what. And reading books and stories that once would have made me snicker or yawn now infected me with a mysterious sadness that would last for hours.

Female hormones at work, dummy, Mary Alice would say.

In my mind I could hear again her taunting voice. She hadn't cushioned her jabs. All right, so a Mary Alice Martinson was one story and a Jody Shepard was another. So what? Didn't the world allow for differences in people? So I *wasn't* into dating yet. Did that immediately label me as some sort of freak?

Well, I didn't feel like a freak. In fact, most of the time I managed to feel pretty good about myself.

Most of the time.

Inching to the side of the bed, I let my gaze travel around the room, hoping it would focus on something in that nine-by-fourteen-foot space that would give a clue to what was stirring inside me.

Except for the new curtains and the flowered wallpaper and the personal stuff I'd accumulated over the past years, not much had happened to it. Which was exactly the way I'd planned on my bedroom staying. And when my mother hinted that *something* should be done to it (a "freshening up" is what she called the massive changes she had in mind), I'd resisted mightily.

My gaze settled on a favorite sight: the snapshots tacked over my dresser. Bob, Benny, Jeremy, and me, the year we were ten, clutching fishing poles and proudly showing off our strings of rainbow trouts. Jeremy and me, sunburned faces peering from the tree house my brother Mike had built in our old elm, mugging like chimps at the camera. Bob Murray and me —

I looked elsewhere:

At my very first fielder's glove, hung at a crazy angle from a hook on one wall. And the beat-up sneaker, which I'd tossed in a corner, hoping to find its mate someday. And my raggedy, outgrown maroon sweat shirt with the sleeves torn off that I couldn't bring myself to use for a dustcloth. And the sun-dried form of a salamander Jeremy had given me the year we were twelve. Cherished specimens, every one.

I stood up and walked toward the dresser mirror. Actually, I'd never had much use for that mirror. When I was a little kid, it was good for staring into only after those occasions when my mother had said, "Jody, kindly remove that smudge from your chin." Which was why it could have made headline news that I, Red

Shepard, was now planted in front of it, peering at my image.

What I saw didn't help.

A mop of carrot-colored hair that shagged unevenly across my forehead. My right cheek-bone sporting a scab from a whack I'd received the week before, trying to snag a fly near second, missing it, and stumbling over the base. And my nose —

That *nose.* I inspected it carefully. Definitely the homeliest nose I'd ever viewed. Didn't fit the rest of my face at all. I stepped back and re-garded what there was of my figure. Per usual, mostly skin covering bones. Except . . . where a girl was supposed to balloon out, and I never had, I now was.

I frowned at my image, then lifted the shag of hair from my forehead and stared at my eyes. Ordinary blue. Very round. *Hmmm.* Sometimes the girls in my class *did* things to their eyes to bring out the color or change the shape. And there must be something a person could buy that would fade freckles. I wondered suddenly what a layered cut would do for my hair. I leaned forward, still frowning — and jerked backward, appalled at what I was thinking. Really, why should it matter to me what I looked like? To the people who'd always counted with me (mainly the other Gophers), I was — well, I *used* to think I was right up there with the rest of them.

I let my sights return to a more comfortable area. The wall that held my old fielder's glove.

I longed, suddenly, to take it down and stroke its smoothness the way I had as a kid.

The glove came from its hook reluctantly. My fingers probed the sagging leather, halted, drew gingerly away. Why hadn't I noticed that jagged rip in the padding before? And when had the leather become so parched?

Was I finally cracking up? I mean, *blubbering over a crummy, broken-down old fielder's glove!* Wow.

Okay, so on the other side of the room sat the salamander, looking very normal. That picked me up. Now, there was a *specimen.* I reached over and grabbed it by its splotched tail.

The tail crumbled in my fingers, disintegrating and sprinkling a coarse gray ash over the rug.

I plucked the remains of tail from the rug and deposited them in the wastebasket. Inside my head a kind of quiet numbness had taken over. I just stood there in the middle of the floor, holding my neck stiffly, not wanting to look anywhere.

Through my partly open window, I could hear the murmur of voices. My mother's and Jeremy's.

Hers was low-pitched, warm, interested in anything Jeremy had to say. Since she'd always considered the kid the greatest happening since the invention of the wheel, this was par for her course. But Jeremy sounded agitated. And when Jeremy got agitated, peculiar things happened to his voice. Squeaky, croaky things. Mom had told him it would pass with time. For his sake, I sincerely hoped so.

I heard my mother say, "Why don't you holler up and ask her?"

There was this silence. Then Jeremy said, sort of hesitating, "Well, if I knew what was bothering her . . ." And then, loud enough to reach past my window: "Red? Hey, Red, are you available?"

I was. I mean, I had no real beef with Jeremy. As for what was bothering me, what could I tell him?

I moved to the window. "Hi, Jeremy," I said in a muffled voice. "What's up?"

"About this afternoon," he said. "Don't you think we should talk it over? Look, if Bob Murray did anything or said anything—"

"I'd rather not discuss it," I said.

"How about dragging down here for a minute and telling me why?"

I thought that over. "Later," I said.

"It's a deal. Phone me when you're ready for a heart-to-heart. And make it kind of soon, will ya? Like, within the next half hour?"

I mumbled something he must have taken for a yes, because he was smiling to himself as he loped across Arbutus Street.

I sat before my dresser mirror for the next half hour, staring at my reflection and brooding. Then, sick of the sight, I got to my feet and marched over to the phone.

And I called up Mary Alice Martinson.

TWO

"Tell me something, Jody," Mary Alice probed thrugh the phone line. "When was the last time you kissed a boy?"

"We-e-ell . . ." I racked my memory. "There was that class hayride, when Hank Benson got absolutely ridiculous and sneaked a kiss while we were all parked out behind Smith's barn, waiting for them to hook up the horses. But that was, *like*"—I shrugged—"nothing. Of course, if you're talking about guys in general, I used to kiss my brother good night. It's a family tradition. Kiss Mom, kiss Dad, kiss Mike—" I heard her snort. "Okay, you're talking about *boys* boys. Well, sometimes when Jeremy and I were little . . ."

"Excluding brothers and household pets."

"Hey, wait a minute," I said, suddenly nettled. "Are you trying to say Jeremy is a—"

"Jeremy is part of your problem. *That's* what I'm trying to say. His constant, juvenile presence is impeding your social progress. Can't you see that, Jody? He's like an overgrown beagle pup. And where Jody goes, the pup is sure to follow."

I resented her describing Jeremy as a beagle pup, hanging around underfoot. Just because we walked to school together, and he was usually waiting for me after school so that we could walk home together, go to baseball practice together, and just plain enjoy each other's company, was no reason to —

"It's obvious he hasn't allowed you to get close enough to any *sophisticated* male long enough to make a dent," she went on. "So if we can just shake Jeremy loose —"

"Now back up," I said. "When you knock Jeremy Barnes, you knock me. I don't want to hurt him."

"So for the present we'll skip the subject of Jeremy." Mary Alice yielded. "But one thing you have to admit — you are in a rut. You're growing up faster than you realize. In a 'girl' way, I mean." Small silence. "And it's beginning to show."

"Oh, for pete's sake, Mary Alice," I exploded, "that is the sappiest —"

"And before you know it, the guys our age and older will begin to notice."

I considered reminding her that she was a year older than me, and a grade higher, and therefore we didn't share the same boy-girl problems. But what would it solve?

"And it wouldn't be a bad idea to bow out of those goofy Arbutus Street Gophers. Jody, do you realize what that does to your image? I mean, playing first base for a sandlot ball team —"

"Shortstop," I corrected.

"Whatever," she said. "The point is, you're not living up to your potential. You have possibilities. With some work here and there, I could really turn you into something. In fact, Arnold Greene and I were discussing it just this morning, and he agreed with me that you could become presentable. I promised him I'd —"

"*Arnold Greene?*" I shrieked. It really shook me. I mean, Arnold was a *senior*. And he had discussed *me*.

"I could start with your hair. It's a beautiful shade of red. But it looks absolutely horrendous the way you have it now. And your eyes aren't bad. Oh, maybe a little blah. But with some blue shadow and a touch of mascara, or even some false lashes. . . . Of course, you realize your nose will take a lot more effort."

By then I'd recovered my voice. And my sanity. "Now, let's get this straight, Mary Alice Martinson," I said firmly. "I have no intention of quitting the Gophers. As for Arnold Greene —"

"So Arnold isn't Mr. Perfection. But he could be a beginning. I suppose I might just as well confess, Jody. Arnold and I talked it over, and he agreed to letting me set up a date with you. A double date. Don and me, Arnold and you. The way I see it, double is safer. At least until you know how to handle yourself. But after that —"

"But *why*?" I wailed. "Did I ask you to —"

"Call it my project for the month," Mary Alice said, sounding pretty pleased with herself.

"Forget it." I tried to dismiss the whole awful idea. "For one thing, my mother would have a fit. She doesn't go for her fourteen-year-old daughter dating," I added, although I had no idea how my mother felt about it, since the subject had never come up.

Mary Alice laughed. "Oh, don't worry about your mother. If there's one thing I know how to do, it's handle mothers." A short pause. Then, "Say, why don't I come over to your house tonight, and we'll get to work on it?"

"But Jeremy is coming over after supper," I said hurriedly. "We're cramming for the earth science exam. Besides, we have to map out the Gophers' schedule."

"*Jeremy*," she said scornfully. "I might've guessed! Well, at least think over what I've been saying, Jody. Look at it this way. It would be an experience. And that's how a person learns. Through experience. Right?"

"I think I hear my mother calling," I said. I mean, lied. "Look, I'll . . . I'll get in touch, Mary Alice. See ya."

Jeremy and I were deep into Earth Science, our semester's homework papers cluttering the dining room table, textbooks opened and passages underlined, wrangling over some sticky points, when Jeremy eased back in his chair, brushed his hair from his eyes, and said quietly, "About what happened this afternoon. I thought you were going to call me, Red. How come you didn't?"

Why was I hesitating to meet his question head on? I'd always been able to lay it on the line with Jeremy. But now I found myself fingering the rim of my Coke glass and groping for words. "Jeremy," I said after a while, "have you ever noticed that I'm — I'm a girl?"

"It has crossed my mind now and then," he said, a tiny smile playing at the corners of his mouth.

"Well, did it ever occur to you that Bob Murray might have a valid point? I mean, obviously he resents the fact that a female has invaded what he considers his territory, and anyone can see he's dying to make it as shortstop."

"He'll recover," Jeremy said mildly. "You've been playing with the Gophers since you were nine, and Bob Murray has managed to suffer through it all these years. Why is it bugging you now, Red?"

I longed to blurt it all out. The jagged pieces of unfamiliar feelings that had invaded my thoughts, refusing to let go, the strange new yearnings that had nothing to do with becoming shortstop for the Gophers. Once, like the day before, I'd have talked it out with Jeremy and listened to his words of reassurance. But for some reason beyond me, my tongue sat in my mouth, volunteering nothing.

"Hey, you know, it's getting kind of late," he said, hopping up from the table and gathering together his papers. "Let's postpone the brain drain until tomorrow, okay?" He eyed me expectantly. "Same time, same place?"

I opened my mouth to say brightly, "Of

course! What else?" What came out was, "I'll let you know, Jeremy."

If he noticed a change, he didn't let on. He just picked up his stuff, put on his lopsided Jeremy-grin, and said, "I'll stop by for you in the A.M. Okay?"

"Sure thing," I said, putting more heartiness in it than I felt, because I'd suddenly experienced . . . *guilt*? But how could that be? I mean, what did I have to feel guilty about?

By morning I was feeling more like my old self. And when Jeremy showed up at the front door, I turned my books over to him to carry (as he'd been doing for so long I actually can't recall when the habit started), and we marched off to school. Together. The way we'd always done.

Jeremy's locker was next to mine. Had been for the past year. His locker worked like a charm. But *mine* — well, the fact is, only Jeremy knew how to get the dumb thing open and closed. A special tap along the metal edge. A kick in a certain spot. A jerk of the handle. Seemed perfectly simple. However, when *I* tried it . . .

Tap, kick, lift. And Jeremy's quick grin. Then he waved and headed for Algebra, and I tried to convince myself there was no real way to avoid Family Living.

Mary Alice Martinson was waiting for me outside the Family Living door. And she was smiling. Mary Alice's mouth doesn't smile easily.

I found myself wanting to back away from that gleeful expression.

"Hey," she said, grabbing my arm. "Good news! I really had to sweat to pull this one off, but wait'll you hear!"

I sneaked a glance toward the Algebra class door. It had just creaked shut behind Jeremy.

"I've arranged something pretty special," she confided, looking smug. "Arnold's willing to go along with it, and I told him you'd be dee-lighted, and — if you turn it down, if you don't say yes . . ." The smugness faded, just for an instant. Then her eyes cleared, as if she knew something about me that I didn't.

I tried to appear disinterested, but the wild thumping against my rib cage must have given me away. Or was my face that transparent?

"As of now, it's set for Saturday night," she said. "Don Petrie and me, Arnold and you, just like I told you. First, out to eat, then to the new flick at the Bijou, and maybe a little dancing afterward. And I'll promise your mother on a stack of Bibles we'll have you home in plenty of time for your beauty sleep. Speaking of beauty . . ."

"Now wait a sec, Mary Alice," I said, hating the shakiness in my voice. "I haven't yet said I'd —"

"Between now and then," she went on, "I'll have to do something about your hair. And you certainly could stand a strong hand with those freckles. There's this new cream that —"

The bell rang. Just in time.

Jeremy and I got together in the cafeteria at lunch, sitting across from each other, exchanging halves of sandwiches and small talk. As usual, we split the dessert both ways.

Between mouthfuls of ham on rye, Jeremy announced that baseball practice would have to be postponed until sometime after Friday's exams. "Then I'll be expecting you out there," he said, darting me a glance. "At your usual stand. Shortstop. I'll pass the word to Bob Murray on that. No hassle from now on."

I bit into the Thursday dessert special, apple kuchen. "Uh, is it definite about our bike hike on Saturday?" I stuck in delicately. After all, we'd planned it for weeks.

He stopped eating and stared at me. "Yeah, sure. Unless it rains or something." Pause. "Why do you ask?"

"Oh, no reason. It's just, well, Mary Alice Martinson had this brainstorm. About going to the movies and stuff. She mentioned double-dating, and I said . . . I mean, I haven't said *yet*—"

"Double-dating? She probably means with her and Don." Jeremy crinkled his nose. "Personally, I consider Mary Alice bad news. For one thing, if she's half as smart as she thinks she is, how come she flunked two courses last term and has to repeat them with us lowly freshmen? But I get along okay with Don. Of course, I haven't done much in the way of dating." He looked a little sheepish. "Actually, I haven't done *any* dating. *But*"—a sudden grin brought his face to life—"well, what the heck, why not? Okay, tell her we'll go."

So how *should* I have explained it? How does an *experienced* person handle a situation like this? Probably very carefully. . . .

"Mary Alice didn't mean *you*," I blurted out. "She was talking about Arnold Greene. And me."

So help me, it just came out that way. I mean, I'd never have *deliberately* done that to Jeremy.

For an instant he did nothing. Then his liquid brown eyes opened wide. "*Arnold Greene?*" His croak rose to a squeak. He must have swallowed a piece of ham or something, because all of a sudden his face turned beet red, and his throat made rapid gulping motions, as if he were having trouble breathing. Then he stood up. "Excuse me," he said in this thick voice. And off he zoomed.

I waited for him until the bell rang. Then I hurried on up to Earth Science, figuring I'd corner him there and get the whole business out in the open. Something I should have done in the first place.

Ordinarily, Jeremy and I sat toward the back of the classroom, where we could whisper and not be caught at it. But today Jeremy was sitting up front, near the teacher. When I came in, he barely glanced up.

I guess there is no way to get somebody's attention if that somebody doesn't want to give it.

At the end of class, Jeremy mixed in with all the other kids making a grand dash for the corridors and walked on ahead of me.

I had a terrible time trying to get my locker open that afternoon. In the end, I had to ask the janitor to come up and work on the stupid thing. Would you believe it took him almost twenty minutes to do what Jeremy could do in five seconds?

THREE

Well, nobody can say I didn't try.

I phoned the Barnes house just after five, wanting to nail Jeremy down on his study plans for the evening. His mother must have hollered his name at least ten times before she finally gave up and told me he was nowhere around. Only after I'd hung up did I see him skulking around his backyard.

He rushed by my house the next morning without even waving to me. And when I met him in a first floor corridor, he loped away before I had a chance to open my mouth. Yet when Arnold Greene came over to my desk in Family Living, guess who peeked into the classroom and glared in our direction?

I missed several things about Jeremy. For one, our head-to-head studying, and my Earth Science exam grade proved it. And that afternoon I missed, even more, Jeremy's chatter, as I made my lonely trek toward Arbutus Street. Then

Arnold drove by in his father's car with Mary Alice and picked me up. And there was Jeremy, his chin on his chest, plodding silently along. He didn't even look up as we zipped past him. "Jeremy is acting like a child," Mary Alice pointed out. "Obviously he's not emotionally ready for dating. Besides," she added, "it's probably a blessing. At least now you'll be free of that millstone around your neck."

My fingers instinctively went to my neck, as if checking for millstones. They came away empty.

"So, okay," Mary Alice said briskly. "First, I'll make my pitch to your mother. Then I'll wave my magic wand and turn you into a Cinderella. Then we'll make the arrangements for Saturday night. There's this new dining spot just outside of town. The Greene Glove. Partly owned by Arnold's uncle, so we can get special rates. And there's the new flick at the Bijou. And then, if you want, we could go to the roller rink. And after *that* . . ." She gave me a slow wink, which I'm sure Arnold must have seen, because he grinned broadly. "Experience," she said. "Remember?"

Speaking of experience, it sure was one, watching Mary Alice zero in on my mother. Although I don't think Mom bought Mary Alice's Miss Sincerity act all the way, she did listen closely to the spiel. And she came to the conclusion that Mary Alice's "double-dating is safer" line had merit. I got the definite feeling my mother wouldn't stand in the way. For some reason, this knowledge depressed me. I think, deep in a chicken part of me, I was counting on her to turn the whole idea down.

And yet, my fear of the unknown was counterbalanced by the heady realization that below that red mop I'd always called my hair, minor miracles were being performed by Mary Alice. I came out of it looking like, well, a girl.

Don Petrie, who had his father's car, picked up Arnold and me. As we eased down our driveway and onto Arbutus, I glanced toward the Barnes house. Not a sign of Jeremy. And his ten-speed bike was gone. I slumped against the car seat. Then I caught Arnold's watchful eye and smiled brightly at him. And we were off.

The Greene Glove. Will I ever feel like anything less than an absolute cretin every time I look back on how I muddied up my brand-new image there?

If only it hadn't been such a *cushy* place! I mean, all those soft lights, and the six-piece string orchestra, and the royal blue carpeting you could sink knee-deep in.

And those waiters, gliding in and out on cats' paws, looking so stuffed-shirt. What must *they* have thought?

I'm a hamburger-with-onion-and-pickle-on-bun person, myself. Order, pay, eat, get out. But at the Greene Glove, you wait. And wait. And wait. Until your stomach starts to growl up a storm, and everybody around you gives you peculiar looks, as if you're a dumb little kid doing that just to embarrass *them*.

And I really don't go for meals with names I can't pronounce that are so heavy with spice, you know you'll be tasting them for days to come. Arnold ordered for both of us, after consulting with me and getting a bewildered "Huh?" Then there was that funny little jar with the stuff in it that looked like catsup that I tipped over on the carpeting. Well, I preferred to think the stain would wash out. But judging by the expression on the waiter's face when he saw it, that ugly red will probably be there for life.

I hadn't *planned* on developing a stomachache. But I did have to take me and my pains to the ladies' room until they let up. Why Mary Alice made such a production out of it is beyond me. Finally everything quieted down inside me, and by the time we were ready to leave for the movies, my stomach felt just fine. I mean, if I was willing to forget what had happened, why wasn't she?

Speaking of the movie: Mary Alice and Don became so engrossed with each other they didn't even know when the picture was over.

As I sat there trying to concentrate on the story, I sensed Arnold moving closer. And when a big smooching scene flashed onto the screen, his arm slid over the back of the seat and rested lightly on my shoulder. My heart pounded away in my chest. Now what? Did he expect the next move to be mine?

I sat up ramrod straight, and after a while his arm worked itself back home.

When the lights came on, Mary Alice uncurled from her cozy position and smoothed down her skirt. "Say, kids," she said. "I have a suggestion. Since it's getting pretty late . . ."

I consulted my watch. It was only nine-thirty.

". . . and I really don't feel up to making it around the rink, why don't we just go for a little night ride?"

"Great idea," Don and Arnold chorused.

I said nothing. But my stomach was churning up a storm again.

Still, I acted pretty cool as I huddled at the far end of the backseat and supposedly gazed out at the dwindling night traffic. Arnold, I could tell, had already made it halfway across the seat.

Mary Alice turned on the car radio, then snuggled up to Don while he tried to drive. In the dimness you could hardly tell where she left off and he began. And next to me, Arnold was humming softly along with the music.

I tensed, preparing for — what? I mean, should I turn slowly and lift my face, like the girl in the big smooch scene? Did I keep my lips closed, or open them just a little? Hold my breath? And what should I do with my nose? Because there it was, just over my mouth — in the way. Should I shut my eyes? Or should I —

"Mary Alice tells me this will be a first for you," Arnold murmured in my ear.

First! Funny, I'd never really dreamed of sharing a kiss with somebody like Arnold Greene. And it had never occurred to me that I'd be worried about what to do with my nose or my eyes. I'd always assumed (when I bothered thinking about it at all) that one day I'd look into *his* (whoever's) eyes, and little bells would go off, and it would just *happen*. But first you had to like the guy. And *trust* him.

I sat up awkwardly, bumping Arnold's chin with my elbow. "I think I'd better go home," I said.

"Home? *Now*?" asked Mary Alice from the front seat. "Aw, come *on*, Jody. Grow up!"

A sound close to a sob escaped from my throat.

There was a silence up front. Then, "Maybe she's not feeling well," Don said. "Remember what happened back at the Glove?" A pause. "Are you sick, Jody?"

Well, my stomach *was* aching, kind of. "Yeah," I said hoarsely.

"Oh, for heaven's sake, let's get the baby home then," Mary Alice snapped.

Arnold was still rubbing his chin. He didn't look at all friendly. He stayed way over on his side.

The trip home was very quiet.

They dropped me off in front of my house. Arnold didn't even bother to get out of the car. Not that I wanted him to.

I spied the gleam of the Barneses' front porch light, and what looked like somebody sitting under it. I decided to scoot across the street, hoping all the while it would be you know who. And sure enough, Jeremy was on the top porch step, just sitting and staring into space. He jumped when he saw me.

I spoke first. "Hi, Jeremy."

A strand of hair had fallen over his puffy eyes,

and there was a dull red spot along his right jawbone, as if he'd been rubbing it. He waved and went back to his staring.

Chancing it, I sat next to him. He didn't move away. After a while he shifted his mournful gaze to me and sighed.

It hurt to see Jeremy looking so down. But I must have appeared less than hilarious myself. I put my hand against his and just held it there, feeling comforted by the warmth. Jeremy didn't say anything, but he sat up straighter.

I really wanted to confess how dumb I felt. Like a little kid who knows she's done something stupid but can't quite put her finger on what. But Jeremy's eyes were clouded over with his private pain. So I just kept my hand on his, hoping he'd get a message from that.

Jeremy, I wanted to ask, *do you ever get a left-out feeling? As if all the other kids your age share a fascinating secret that you don't?*

But he kept on staring, not reading my mind at all.

I concentrated, longing to let him know yet not up to stating it out loud. *Jeremy, do you sometimes have the sneaking suspicion you'll be the last kid in your crowd to catch on? And by the time you finally get the drift, the rest of the gang will have left you behind in the dust?*

What I did manage to get past my suddenly tight throat was, "Jeremy, if you've been dying to ask how that double date turned out"—I glared his way in the semidarkness—"all I can tell you is *don't ask*."

There was a little silence. And then, "Well, how about that," Jeremy said, so softly I could barely hear him. I think he was smiling. But I wasn't up to pushing an investigation.

We sat there for a long minute, just breathing the night air. Then Jeremy said, "Red?"

I turned, catching an odd expression in his brown eyes. He hesitated, as if reaching for words. "I just wanted to tell you . . ." He cleared his throat. "I'm calling a practice session for Monday afternoon. Think you can make it?"

"Without a doubt," I said.

We sat there for a while longer, hugging our own thoughts. I was pretty comfortable with mine. Jeremy and I were friends again. The same old friends we'd always been. Nothing had changed between us.

But I was wrong. In subtle ways, changes had already altered what Jeremy and I had going for us. And others were in the works. Little did either of us suspect that night that we'd never again be the same old Jeremy and Red.

FOUR

The next afternoon began uneventfully, easing along like any other Sunday around our establishment. Jeremy had ambled over after dinner and was making himself at home on our creaky porch glider, while leafing through the sports section of my father's Sunday *Times*. I was perched not far from him, with half an eye trained on the front screen door, trying to appear less than interested in the action going on behind it.

Said action being what my brother Mike and his girl friend Gail were up to on the living room loveseat. She'd been invited for dinner, and anyone could tell she could hardly wait for the meal to get finished so they could sprint to that little sofa. And as soon as Mom and Dad wandered over to the neighbors, things came to life in there, starting with Mike's soft laughter and a burst of giggles from Gail.

My ears zeroed in on the screen door, trying to sort out those interesting sounds. Since Mike and Gail were all of eighteen — seniors at Wilmont High — and had a track record of several romances apiece, it seemed safe to suppose they'd have a few more answers about, well, Life than I did. But then, didn't everybody? I mean, any half-smart *fifth-grader* would know more than I did.

"What d'you think of the Mets' chances this year?" Jeremy asked suddenly, hauling his nose from the sports section. "My personal opinion is . . ."

I was craning my neck trying to follow some new sounds in there.

". . . is maybe the Dodgers and the Mets will get together and fly on the backs of the Houston Astros to the moon," he said offhandedly. "What's your opinion, Red?"

"I, uh . . ." I brought my eyes back to Jeremy. And, I guess, blushed.

"If you've developed a thing for watching mushy stuff," Jeremy put in, "you ought to come over to our house around ten, most Friday nights. You'll learn more from my sister Victoria and her guy Jack than you'll ever want to know."

"Oh, I wasn't —"

"Maybe it wouldn't hurt to drop the spy act long enough to concentrate on picking up your crummy Earth Science grade," he said, folding up the sports section and laying it on the glider. "And of course you know how . . ." He let that hang in midair.

A clear invite to bike hike among the back road rock piles, searching out some fossil remains to pacify our teacher. With Mr. Ames, extra projects counted.

The boy had a point. "Great. I'll run down a parent and leave a message," I said, standing up and fighting a yawn. "If you'll dig out your pick hammer, I'll adjust the gearshift on my ten-speed and find a knapsack."

I was interrupted by the arrival of my father, plodding across our lawn, heading for the back door.

One thing about Dad: There's nothing wrong with his eyesight. Or his vocal chords.

Personally, I'd have been a little embarrassed — I mean, a lot embarrassed — if my father had come up to *me* and some guy and barked (in a voice guaranteed to crack timber), "Okay, you two, let's break it up! Out of the living room!"

But Mike and Gail merely stood up and grinned foolishly at each other and sauntered off to the kitchen to make baloney sandwiches. Maybe that's what comes of having a track record like theirs. You get kind of used to being thrown out of living rooms.

I tried to discuss this with Jeremy as we rolled out of town. But at the moment, his mind seemed taken up with other thoughts. Like who was going to start at what position on the Gophers. And the type of trilobite fossil certain to thrill Mr. Ames's flinty heart. And how invigorating it was to move those old wheels along the terrain, eating up the miles, enjoying the rustic scenery, breathing in that glorious, pure air. I mean, it seemed a shame to break into his upbeat mood with my trivia.

Okay, so he didn't come through with answers to certain questions. Like what guys *really* thought of girls who didn't mind necking with them on a loveseat. And why my brother Mike considered it such a big deal to brag about "scoring."

Matter of fact, I wasn't dead sure what "scoring" meant. I did drop that word experimentally into the conversation as we rode along, placing it (rather cleverly, I thought) between Benny Armand's creative line of patter from behind his catcher's mask and Dave Lansing's curveball that cut the inside corner sharp as a new blade.

"Scoring?" Jeremy echoed, his face innocent. "You mean our team's, or the other guy's?"

So much for trivia.

For a while we hugged the shoulder of the paved highway almost in silence, with Jeremy in the lead. It turned out he wasn't personally familiar with the road and where it would take us. According to Jeremy, Benny had once explored the area and discovered a whopper of a trilobite. That was *it*, for previous knowledge. And as the green meadows and dandelions and leafy trees faded out, and long stretches of brush and scrubby, old pines faded in, I began to feel uneasy.

Suddenly from nowhere great chunks of elephant-colored rock zoomed in. Broken shelves of it hung over the road, and pieces had come loose and were littering the shoulder.

"You can't trust the shale rock out here," I warned Jeremy hoarsely. "It must be a trillion years old. And look, some of it's crumbling."

"Thanks for bringing it to my attention," Jeremy muttered, speeding up a little, away from me.

"And if you'll also notice," I announced to his flannel-shirted back, "your civilized county highway has just developed a split personality." I pointed to the right and left forks. Both gravel.

Which meant a choice. Go home and forget the whole thing. Which, being us, we wouldn't. Take the right (winding around a bend, leading to who knew where). Take the left (sloping down to what looked like the remains of a riverbed).

Jeremy stopped his bike and rested his chin on the handlebars. "Benny did say something about a fork. I think he said turn right at the fork. . . ." His gaze shifted. He frowned. "Or did he say *left*?"

Mentally I flipped a coin. "I'll opt for the left," I decided.

In such wacky ways are decisions sometimes made. Now and then I wonder how our lives might have been different if we hadn't acted on my so-called impulse. For one thing, we wouldn't have scrambled down to that riverbed and pick-hammered our way through the shale to the limestone and released from its eons-old prison this huge, almost flawless trilobite. And then we wouldn't have gotten courageous enough to explore the nearby woods, and we wouldn't have come to the remains of what had once been a house.

There wasn't much left. Shreds of cement clinging to some weathered brick where the foundation had stood. A rusted-out kitchen sink. Two battered cooking pots. A section of bed springs. Just enough to let us know that somebody had lived there a long time ago.

And enough to jog my memory. "Hey, Jeremy," I said. "Remember when we were about seven, and we played house in your backyard? We'd line up my dolls and make them our kids, and —"

"And I'd shape twine into squares, to lay out the rooms." Jeremy took it from there. "And we'd stick a lawn chair where our pretend living room was and put your toy stove in our kitchen." He caught my eye and grinned.

"We can at least use the dining room here," I said, reading his mind and reaching into the knapsack, "because I brought along some egg-salad sandwiches and stuff, plus this thermos of hot chocolate. So maybe if we lay a jacket down next to these old bricks . . ."

Jeremy took off his new spring jacket and spread it carefully on the ground, just inside the foundation line, while I fished around in the knapsack, coming up with the sandwiches, a package of M & M's, and the thermos.

We split the sandwiches and M & M's and shared the thermos cup. And when the hot chocolate spilled onto Jeremy's new jacket, he took the blame for it. Said he'd accidentally jiggled my elbow. Funny, I didn't notice the jiggling.

In a way I couldn't quite understand, that was the most satisfying meal we'd shared in a long time. After we'd finished, while Jeremy did what he could for his jacket, I sat back against a mound of bricks and smiled to myself, feeling good all over.

Jeremy and I were in no hurry to leave. For one thing, he seemed in the mood to gab. Just like old times. And I didn't mind listening one little bit.

Somehow, we got onto the subject of his seventeen-year-old sister Victoria and the fuss she was kicking up in the Barnes family structure. "It's Jack Parsons." Jeremy launched into the details. "Vicky's real hung up on the guy. And he's made himself practically a permanent fixture at our house. Which would be okay, if he didn't take advantage of the situation. What I mean is, sometimes, well, like when my folks go away for the evening . . ." Jeremy glanced at me from the corner of his eye. "Ma says she's not blind, and if it goes on much longer at the present speed, Vicky's headed for big trouble. But Vicky figures —"

"Trouble?" I sat up straight. "What kind of trouble?" My brain raced through all the possible kinds of trouble Victoria could get into.

"Oh, *you* know." Jeremy waved his hand vaguely. "I think Pop's pretty worried." He looked away from me. "But since they'd rather it not be discussed outside the family, maybe I'd better not . . ."

"Aw, come on, Jeremy," I coaxed, "I'm like family. And you know I'd never blab."

"Hey," Jeremy yelped, jumping to his feet, "do you see what I see? The sun's starting to go down. We'll be skinned alive if we don't get on out of here!"

I suppose I could have quarreled with his timing. But there was no denying that sun. As I looked, it slipped behind a large, gray cloud, cooling the air just enough to make me wish I'd brought my heavy jacket. We didn't waste a minute getting out of there.

As we wheeled back onto the paved road, a wind blew up from nowhere, chilling me to the bone. Jeremy, who was in the lead, didn't seem to feel it. He'd returned to being gabby, rattling on about this and that (bypassing the subject of Victoria) as we rolled along. Snatches of his end of the conversation flicked by my ears.

"What do you say next Saturday we make another run to the left fork? Next time we can bring a regular lunch and some root beer, and maybe start a litle earlier, dig awhile in the bedrock, then just laze around and talk. I mean, this was the most fun we've had in a long, long . . . hey, *Red*! What thinkest thou?"

I came to. "Huh? Oh. Uh, yeah, Jeremy. Fine. Fine with me." But after a little listening, I lapsed back into my own thoughts. About Victoria, for one thing. And Jack. And all the inside information I didn't have about what goes on after the parents leave for the evening and a girl and guy are left alone. Of course, when Jeremy and I were left alone after hours, what happened was maybe we'd scare up a game of table tennis down in the cellar. Or work on a jigsaw puzzle. Or follow a ballgame on TV and argue about who'd win. Funny, it had always seemed plenty good enough before.

". . . And, boy, wait till old Ames gets a load of that trilobite! Makes Benny's look like a shrimpy nothing. . . ." (Rabbit scooting in front of bikes — temporary holdup.) "Look, Red, I'll leave the knapsack on your front porch, where you'll spot it first thing and remember to bring it. But who's kidding who? After all our work getting it,"— ha-ha from Jeremy —"there's no way you'll forget. Right? Bet Ames will up your mark at least ten —" The rest of it was lost in the breeze.

Jeremy kept up this line of patter all the way home. His voice floated behind him, rising and falling, blending with the late afternoon air. I kept this terribly interested expression on my face (just in case he happened to turn around and look) and made noises I sincerely hoped came through like conversation. But my thoughts were drifting back to what had happened the night before. My so-called social fling. It was spelled D-I-S-A-S-T-E-R. If I had it to do over again . . . but why quibble about what I'd do? Mary Alice had no doubt washed her hands of me. *Let's get the baby home*, she'd snapped. And the expression on her face had said the rest. I was hopeless. A basket case.

At the corner where Lincoln Avenue meets Arbutus, Jeremy slammed on his brakes. Not the brightest thing he'd ever done. I missed, by a hair, ramming into the back of his ten-speed.

Naturally, I was jarred awake. And jarred in

other ways. I don't take kindly to acts of stupidity that cause near-accidents. And I was all wound up to tell him so.

Jeremy was just sitting there, his elbows propped on the handlebars, staring into space. And something about the set of his shoulders told me to wait him out.

I should have guessed, by the redness taking over his ears and the accusing expression in his eyes, what was to come. Accusing expressions make me uncomfortable. Especially when I'm not sure which horrible crime I'm supposed to have committed.

"Do you realize"— Jeremy had to force his words through his teeth —"that for the past fifteen minutes you have not said one sensible thing to me?"

Some crime! I almost laughed out loud.

"In fact," he enlarged on his injuries, "I don't think you were listening to a word I said!"

"Hey, that's not fair," I flared back. "I certainly *was*." Was what? Listening? To every word?

He stared at me through brooding eyes. "Something here is not what it was," he muttered. "Something's changed. I know it. I can feel it. Maybe it's something *I* did." He sat up straight. "Hey, that's the trouble — isn't it, Red? You're sore at me. I did something, or *said* something."

"That has to be the silliest statement you *ever* —"

"Yeah, I guess that does sound pretty sappy." Jeremy's mouth made a sheepish grin. "It's just, well, you and me, we go back a long way. We're buddies. But sometimes I get to thinking one day you'll look at me and say, 'Ugghh, what a jerk!' Okay, so maybe I shouldn't let it bug me. There are plenty of other guys to hang around with, if you want to call it quits. But the fact is, Red, it does bug me. I *like* what we have going for us." The grin slid up to his eyes. "Or does that sound sappy, too?"

I swallowed past a funny place in my throat. "No way, pal," I said. "No way."

We finally made it home. Jeremy dumped the knapsack on my front porch, then hitched himself back up on the ten-speed. He did his farewell wave bit and put on his good old ear-to-ear grin. "See ya, Red. Tomorrow A.M. and after school at Gopher practice. Right?"

"Right," I said.

I stood on our porch steps and, as I'd done so many times over the years, watched Jeremy make it across Arbutus and onto his own front porch.

In our house it takes time to get to the more fulfilling activities. First you have to wade through endless Sunday evening chores—straighten the living room, separate your laundry from the rest of the gang's, scrape the supper dishes, clear the table, stand by with dishtowel in hand while Mom goes into her suds-and-rinse routine. Fun, fun, fun.

Finally, at eight-thirty, I headed for my room.

Although not without some flak from my dad. "But, Jody," he said, glancing up from his *TV*

Guide, "isn't this just a little early for you? You haven't gone to bed at eight-thirty since you were ten."

"Uh, the bike hike," I said, trying to appear slightly frayed at the edges. "Guess it did me in. My legs . . ." I sort of shuffled toward the stairway, stopping to rub at my right knee.

"Your *legs*?" His eyebrows shot up to here. "At your age, those legs should take any kind of punishment short of being sawed in half." And then, spotting something he'd been waiting to see on TV, he dismissed me with, "Oh, well, kid, hobble off to bed."

I sat on the edge of my bed, wanting to stretch out and go to sleep, yet knowing what I had to do. Sleep would have to wait. The time had come for Red Shepard to pull herself together and plunge into some new-line thinking.

My eyes caught the open bedroom door. I got up and closed it, reconsidered, then reached out and carefully locked my door. I moved back to the four-poster.

"Jody?" My mother's voice sounded from just beyond the bedroom door.

I sat as still as I could, barely breathing.

Outside, there was silence. And then, a knock. "Jody, are you awake?"

Maybe if I made gentle snoring noises, she'd figure I was asleep and leave.

Mom tried the door. "She's locked it," I could hear her say. And then, "That's odd. Jody's never locked her door before." After a minute she went away.

Leaving me no alternative but to do what I'd

said I would do.

I supposed I could start with my room. Begin with sensible things. Like, get rid of that sock and the old plaid sneaker gathering dust in the corner. Junk the maroon sweat shirt. Give away the battered fielder's glove to some young kid who wouldn't mind the aging leather and a rip in the padding. Do something about those obsolete snapshots tacked over the dresser.

Red Shepard and her little pals. There they hung in all their glory, smiling down so winningly. Bob Murray, Benny, Jeremy, and me. Jeremy and me. Bob and me.

Bob and me. I moved closer, eyeing that one. A dumb thing to do. I mean, who was he, after all? Just one of the guys. And a jerky one, at that. Nobody very special.

I lifted away the snapshots. Two of them resisted. I tore a corner off Jeremy and me, and badly crinkled Benny's left arm. But Bob Murray came loose like a charm.

I smoothed out the damaged snapshots and stuck them in a dresser drawer. For a long minute I studied the picture of Bob and me. He had a good nose, I had to admit. At least, better than mine, although his ears were a little funny-shaped. But then they did fit that strong jawline. As for his eyes . . .

As I've mentioned, sometimes I act on impulse. At least I can't think of one other reason why I would find two new tacks and put the snapshot of Bob Murray and me back up on the wall. This time, closer to my bed.

FIVE

Jeremy got to our house a little early Monday morning. Plenty early for all I had to do before we left for school. From where I sat (glued to the chair before my mirror), I could hear him roaming around downstairs, helping himself to some toast, whistling tunelessly, then settling down in front of our TV, taking in the *Today* show. During the commercials, he would get up and stand at the bottom of the stairway, making noises I was supposed to interpret as *Come on, Red, what's the holdup?* But my hands were full, frantically trying to perform the magic on my hair that Mary Alice had done with no effort. When you have ten thumbs where others have just two, nothing very magical is apt to happen. To make matters worse, a small red dot under my left ear had erupted into Mount Vesuvius. I dabbed on some medicated glop, hoping for a miracle. A hopeless hope.

Still, I did have my small triumphs.

I came down the stairs slowly, feeling just a little shy about what I'd accomplished. Not that Jeremy would actually notice. He had never been big on noticing. Noticing *that* sort of accomplishment, I mean.

"Hey," he said, getting to his feet. "You look . . ." He frowned. "Got on new jeans, or something?"

"Try again," I said, blinking my eyes. The glued-on lashes Mary Alice had forgotten to take home with her swept satisfyingly across my vision. When I go for something, I go all-out. And lashes were that week's "something."

"Oh, yeah," Jeremy muttered. "The eyes." The noise coming from his mouth sounded suspiciously like a snicker.

I stood very still and pretended my face was made of concrete.

"Where'd you get those?" he asked from behind the hand he'd placed over his mouth.

I feathered a finger along my lashes. "You mean, *these*?"

Jeremy's hand came away. And whatever snicker he had left he'd stuffed away somewhere. "Not bad," he said politely. "Except . . ." He hesitated. Then, "But I would advise removing them before we go to practice this afternoon. The other guys, well, you know how the guys are. They might . . ."

"Laugh?" I put it delicately.

Jeremy let that one ride. But the tips of his ears had enough sense to turn beet red.

"Well, what are we standing around here for?" I said, suddenly irritated. "Are we going to school, or are we not?" And sweeping past him, I gathered up my own books and marched to the front door.

We were halfway down the sidewalk when Jeremy croaked, "Hey, where's the trilobite? Don't tell me you *forgot*?"

So who could remember everything?

When Jeremy came back, lugging our fossil, he was still growling to himself. I caught some words. Pointed remarks about me, and about girls in general. I chose to ignore them. But for Jeremy and me, the walk to school was remarkably empty of conversation.

By lunch period, however, we'd recovered the lost art. Jeremy was chatting along as if nothing out of the ordinary had been uttered. And I was feeling pretty good about a couple of things. Like the approving nod from Mary Alice when I walked into Family Living. And the *wow!* glance from one of the goof-offs — Marty Keegan — lining the window side of the room, as if he were holding back a low wolf whistle by the skin of his teeth. (I'd also worked at trying to catch Bob Murray's eye. No go. Just couldn't do it.) But when Marty broke down and smiled in my direction, I automatically reached up to check out Mount Vesuvius, then slid my fingers away and thought, *So what?* and smiled back.

Anyway, Jeremy and I had split the Monday special (a slab of corned beef on pumpernickel, spiced up with fancy sauce) and were working on our orange chiffon pie, and I was letting Jeremy ramble on, trying to look vitally interested. Which ordinarily is no chore. I mean, I *enjoy* listening to him run through his life experiences. Jeremy has the neatest talent for hyping up the most *nothing* trials and tribulations. And that noontime he was really wound up. But for some reason I couldn't seem to concentrate.

". . . and as I was telling the President, when he stopped by to ask my advice," my wandering ears picked up from Jeremy's monologue, "the best way to handle the Middle East situation is . . ."

"President? Middle East?" I caught his watchful eye. "Oh, *you*."

There was a pause. Then Jeremy said, "And how was *your* morning?"

I debated. But not for long. "Jeremy," I said, "do you consider me, oh, physically attractive?"

Jeremy pushed back from his chiffon pie and cocked his head like a bird. "I suppose. Like they say, you'll do."

"Of course, it could be the lashes," I confided. I blinked hard, testing the adhesive. Still there. "But this guy in Family Living, I think he noticed. Me. My eyes. Whatever. Not that it matters one way or the other," I tacked on, suddenly uneasy about how I must be coming across. "But —"

"Guy? What guy?"

"Oh, nobody terribly exciting. Just . . . well, okay, if you must know, Marty Keegan."

"*Marty?*" Jeremy opened his mouth so wide I could count every bicuspid. They probably could hear his laughter clear down to the boiler room.

I waited for Jeremy to calm down to hiccups. And then I turned on the internal chill, full force.

He wiped off what was left of his grin and put a hand on my arm. "Hey, Red, I wasn't laughing at *you*. What I'm trying to tell you is, Marty broke the nosepiece to his specs during first period gym. And the guy's blind as a bat without them." Jeremy patted my arm, as if wanting to console me. "So if you thought he was maybe smiling at you, or giving you the eye . . ."

So much for glued-on lashes.

After lunch, Jeremy did his tap-kick-lift to my locker and removed the triolobite, handling it with exquisite care. As if that prehistoric lobster were rare, hand-blown glass. And when he set it on Mr. Ames's desk, you could see pride bursting from every pore.

"An extra project, Jeremy?" Mr. Ames asked. "Very nice. Although, with your A+ on the exam, I am a little surprised —"

"It's not mine," Jeremy cut in quickly. "I'm just, uh, delivering it for . . ." He jerked a thumb in my direction and his ears flamed red.

Mr. Ames stared at me over the top of his horn-rims. "Oh? Fine," he said. His facial expression said, "That'll be the day."

Somebody snickered as I plodded up the aisle to my seat. And Bob Murray, showing all his teeth in a grin, leaned my way. "Hold it, Red," he whispered, just loud enough. "I do believe you're shedding." He pointed to my right cheek.

From which dangled a tiny, feathery object.

As Mary Alice instructed me later, the *couth* response to that would be to shrug it off. Blink. Smile. Maybe remove the other lash and wave it in the air, playing for laughs.

So I muffed it. Lucky for me the other kids' interest had shifted to the trilobite. The second lash had loosened and was working itself onto the tip of my nose. Who needed an audience for *that* big rescue scene?

Fortunately only Bob Murray was glancing my way, grinning for dear life. Which wouldn't have been so irritating (I mean, I could have blamed his grin on a hundred other things), if he hadn't leaned toward me and whispered, "Need any help with that, Red?"

I doubled up my fists, mentally ready to belt him one, when I, well, I noticed his teeth. He'd had his braces removed the November before. Why had it taken me so long to discover the whiteness, the straightness of Bob's teeth, and the great things they did for the rest of his face?

And it was remarkable what time could do for some people, in other ways. Back in the third grade, Bob Murray had been half a head shorter than I was. And skinny, with a squeaky little voice. Somewhere along the line he'd become a healthy-looking hulk, with muscles to spare. And his voice had become deep. Bass. Most of the time.

All this I noted while picking up a pencil I'd accidentally dropped. With a little luck and a few more fumbles of the pencil, who knew what I'd see?

Mr. Ames called me over to his desk. "Jody,"

he said, "since Jeremy has given you almost all the credit for this really superior specimen, I'll go along with raising your semester grade to a C+."

Which gives a clue as to the spectacular grade I'd been saddled with until then. Still, giving me "almost all the credit" had to be a gross exaggeration of the truth, in any language. Jeremy had spotted the trilobite nesting in the bedrock, and he'd done most of the digging. I opened my mouth, about to blurt something out, when Jeremy caught my eye, frowned, and shook his head. So I concentrated on attempting to look properly modest. Which didn't take much acting skill. I had plenty to be modest about.

At the end of the class period, as we all filed out, I managed to break into line behind Bob Murray — tripping over something or other, lurching into him. Accidentally, of course. So why he wheeled around and scowled, muttering a nasty crack about dumb girls and their clodhopper feet, was beyond me. Ordinarily, he'd have heard from me, loud and clear. But for some reason, the words stuck in my throat. And I just stood there like a big ninny, with my lower lip hanging out a mile. Pout, is what I did. Not my usual speed at all.

Jeremy caught up with me at our lockers. He was breathing extra hard. Trying to catch up with me when I'm agitated will do that. "Hey, Red," he got out between breaths, "why didn't you wait up when I hollered?"

I knew he was waiting for some sort of explanation. But I was having trouble enough trying to explain me to myself.

Other words were on the tip of his tongue; I could almost reach out and touch them. But Jeremy just let the words dangle, while he scratched his ear and finally managed to say, "Uh, you are coming to Gopher practice this afternoon, aren't you?"

"Of course," I said. Curtly. Why curtly? Why anything? I had no ready answers.

"Pick you up around four?"

I shrugged. And watched glumly while he did his tap-kick-lift to my locker. As we clumped down the stairway to the first floor exit, we exchanged the briefest of conversations. Halfway down the stairs, Jeremy hesitated and eyed me cautiously. "You okay?" he asked. "Certainly," I snapped back. He looked hurt. "Just asking," he mumbled. And we walked, in silence, down the rest of the stairs.

I felt like a rat. I mean, why was I taking my peculiar mood out on Jeremy (who was, after all, my best friend)? Well, I'd soon remedy that. I'd gab so much during the trek homeward, and to the sandlot, the kid would be sick unto death of my voice.

"So who asked you to turn into a talking machine?" Jeremy cut through my chatter as we got within sight of the Gopher playing lot. "What I'm saying is, you're not acting your usual self. And there has to be a reason. Listen, Red, if it's not something *I* said, could it be one of the *other* guys—" He stopped in his tracks.

"Hey, when we were coming out of Earth Science, didn't I see Bob Murray yakking with you? Or, more like, growling? Didn't catch his message, but the facial expression was sure familiar. We both know how Bob can sound off. And he's been acting pretty stupid about that shortstop thing. If he said anything rotten —"

"It is not anything Bob Murray said!" Although why I felt I had to deny it that explosively, I wasn't sure. A quiet wisecrack followed by a who-cares laugh would have been plenty sufficient.

"Okay, okay." Jeremy cut it short. "So we'll drop the subject. For now. But just for the record, let me say this, one last time. You are the Gophers' shortstop. And no matter what anybody — Murray included — thinks, you will *stay* the Gophers' shortstop." He held my gaze with his. "Have I made myself clear?"

I nodded. Why not? I mean, at that particular moment I'd have let Jeremy believe the moon was made of green cheese, if that had been his hang-up. But all sorts of wheels were spinning like mad inside my head.

The rest of the team had already straggled onto the field by the time Jeremy and I got there. Dave Lansing, who nursed high hopes of making starting pitcher, was on the mound, trying out his breaking curve. He zeroed in a good one to Benny Armand, who was crouched behind home plate, reaching, connecting, building up a sweat under his catcher's mask. Neither of them paid us the slightest attention as we huddled along the sideline and watched.

Concentration, and a burning desire to make it. Dave and Benny could have invented those traits. *Once*, I thought wistfully, *I was like that. Once, like a week ago.*

Bob, working on his batting stance along the first base line, was hefting two bats. He dropped one and sliced viciously at the air with the other. Then he glanced up and saw Jeremy and me. Or should I say, just me? Because that tantalizing grin came back, and he said, "Well, well, our dear little shortstop did show up after all. Figured you'd still be in front of a mirror, glueing on your phony eyelashes." And then he laughed. One of those laughs that doesn't sound at all amused.

"Just ignore him," Jeremy advised from behind his hand.

Well, I'd try. But a little voice inside my head told me that wouldn't be so easy. I looked quickly away from Bob, not caring to alert him, or anyone else, to the confusion of emotions that was bubbling inside me.

But even as Jeremy and I gave him the cold shoulder and sauntered across the sandlot field, my eyes played traitor, sneaking a peek at Bob.

Dumb little questions flitted through my brain. Like, why had I put on the brand-new purple sweat shirt with the velvety nap that fit me like a second skin and showed off areas previously left to the male imagination? And why had I fashioned those corkscrew curls along each side of my face, long enough to hide the disgusting eruption under my left ear? I'd always considered that type of curl too cutsy-poo for words, not my style at all. And why should I care at all what Bob — or any of the guys — thought? In theory, I was there to play sandlot ball. And to prove myself the best darned shortstop in our sectional league.

We settled into position on the field. Jeremy had penciled us in for pop flies to the outfield and some more work on our double-play technique. Then we'd try a few innings of straight ball and see how we'd muddle through.

I watched with grudging admiration as Bob Murray commandeered the balls that Joey Michaels slugged out to center field. No doubt about it, the boy was sharp. I'd always prided myself on my speed. But Bob made me look strictly leadfoot. He was over there and under the ball exactly when he should have been, and his throws to the infield were strong and true. He could easily become the best thing to happen to our team that season. Would his quickness and sense of timing do even more for the Gophers if Bob somehow made it to shortstop?

I bided my time. The double-play session should prove something. I'd worked on it so many times I could go through the motions backward.

No doubt if I'd been concentrating I'd have seen the ball. As it was, I could barely see at all from my position on the ground, with my nose buried in second base. But the throw from third had been so . . . *swift.*

At least, that's what I told Jeremy, who helped me to my feet and walked me to our makeshift dugout. The bump on my head wasn't much. Just a little crease over the right eye where the ball had briefly connected. Over the years I'd picked up a slew of those head jobs — and I'd brushed myself off and gone back to playing. This time . . .

"Gee, is it that bad?" Jeremy croaked, hovering over me, looking anxious. He handed me a crinkled hanky from his back pocket. I mopped at my streaming eyes. "Maybe if you rested a minute."

I let all my bones sag to the turf. The other kids wandered over and stood around, uneasy, not knowing how to react. They weren't used to Red Shepard showing pain.

"I'll be okay after a while," I said, sending up my basset hound expression. "In the meantime, why don't you guys go back to the field and work on the double play? One of you could fill in at shortstop. Like, maybe Bob could come out of center field." I could feel Jeremy's eyes narrow at me. But (as he'd said himself) some things are best left ignored.

"Why, sure, Red," Bob's voice came through eagerly. "Glad to fill in for you. Any time." Then, less eagerly, "I mean, until you feel up to it." So what if I knew what he was *really* thinking? Wasn't that what I'd been counting on? Bob Murray's yen to take over?

Jeremy stuck around after the others had scattered and were reassembling on the field. He hunched forward, jutting his face close to mine.

"Red, sometimes I don't understand you at all," he whispered. "The guy's been eyeing your position from the beginning. And now you're practically *handing* it over." He straightened abruptly, suspicion hoarsening his whisper. "Am I reading this right? You're doing it on purpose? You *want* —"

"Hey, *Barnes*!" From the mound, where Dave Lansing was winding up to throw. "You want me to feed him the slow curve, or should I zing in my fastball?"

Jeremy's lips came together. His jawline tightened. Lurching to his feet, he plodded back onto the field, where he immediately began to bark out orders to Dave and Benny and to decide who should hang in where. Another side to Jeremy. All business.

I knew it would hurt, but I didn't realize how much until I watched Bob Murray turn my spot at shortstop into something horribly close to perfection. Speed, grace, timing. He had them all.

Okay, so which law said I had to sit there and suffer silently? Nobody had to clue Red Shepard in to the handwriting on the wall!

I fumbled around for my infielder's glove, got up carefully, and eased into the background. And when the noise and hustle reached a certain crescendo, I quietly moved what was left of me on out of there.

SIX

Mary Alice was waiting on our front porch, almost as if she'd *expected* me to walk out on the Gophers and drag home to lick my wounds.

One thing for sure: I hadn't intended giving her the edge by blurting out what happened. But Mary Alice Martinson has a positively demonlike talent for worming information from people. And, in all honesty, I wasn't exactly operating at my sharpest.

"Good," she said, looking smug. "In fact, perfect! Now that you've given the boot to that tribe of permanent juveniles, Jody Shepard can begin to *live*."

"Hold it," I said, exasperated, peeved, outraged, you name it. "Stop right *there*. When you knock the Gophers, you knock —"

"Speaking of knocking," Mary Alice cut in, "why don't you knock that line off? You've chewed it about to death. Don't get me wrong, Jody. Loyalty to your old chums is a fine thing.

But let's face it, where has it gotten you? Socially speaking, you're a walking disaster. I tried my level best the other night to turn you around and guide you into —"

"Some guide," I sniffed. "Into the waiting hands of Arnold Greene. If that's progress, who needs it?"

"Ah, yes. Arnold." Mary Alice sighed. "I suppose we'd better discuss him." She eyed our porch glider, then plunked herself into it and patted the space next to her. A clear invite to join her and pick apart A. Greene.

Well, I wasn't up to it. The truth is, parts of *me* felt as if they'd already been picked apart, bone by bone.

"Arnold," Mary Alice went on anyway, "was possibly an unfortunate choice for first-time dating." If she was waiting for a sign of life from me, she didn't get one. "By that, I mean he's shy about dating girls his own age. My personal theory is they make him feel inadequate. With good reason. The painful fact is, Arnold Greene isn't exactly considered Mister Super Cool by the senior girl set, and he knows it. On the other hand, young, untried kids like you make him feel secure about his masculinity. So when I reminded him you were only fourteen and hadn't begun to date, naturally he jumped at the chance. Now if you want my personal assessment —"

"I don't *need* your personal assessment!"

"I think you should date someone closer to your age-level and social experience. A boy you could be attracted to, given a slight assist by a more with-it person like me. The question is, who?"

I made an unrefined noise with my mouth.

Mary Alice pursed her lips and looked thoughtful. "I suppose, if worse comes to worst, you could start with one of those unkempts on your sandlot team. At least you'd feel comfortable with a Gopher, and it would be a first step, until you're ready for a *real* guy. So think it over, Jody, and when you've come up with somebody acceptable —"

I opened my mouth.

"And, by acceptable, I do not mean Jeremy Barnes! We both know how impossible that *child* would be."

I closed my mouth.

"Now, let's make a quick rundown of the team. There's Joey Michaels, of course. But he's really such a *kid*. Sandlot baseball is all the boy knows, and if he doesn't wake up and smell the coffee, that's all he'll ever know. So scratch *him*. Okay, then there's . . ."

Bossy, insensitive, takeover artist. Otherwise known as Mary Alice Martinson. Why was I even giving Miss Lovely the time of day? "Let's drop it right here, Mary Alice." I backed away and pointed myself toward the front door. "I have a million important things to do."

"Say, what about Bob Murray? He, at least, has possibilities, right?"

My fingers automatically came away from the doorknob.

"He's presentable. The braces are off his teeth,

and he must have grown six inches in the past year, and, okay, let's face it, Bob's a very good-looking guy. In fact, if I weren't going steady right now . . ." Her voice dropped, and she glanced around, as if expecting Don Petrie to materialize on our doorstep.

"Surely" — I sank in the needle — "you wouldn't consider hanging out with one of the unkempts."

"Oh, I wouldn't call *Bob* . . ." Mary Alice suddenly looked uncertain. A first for her. "I mean, don't you agree he's operating on a higher level? Any day now that boy will be over the boisterous, little-kid stage. And when he is, some lucky girl will be . . ."

I let her run out of words all by herself.

"But we're talking about *you*," she finally remembered. "And the way I see it, as long as Bob Murray's still on the available list, we can fit him into your scene without much trouble. Naturally we'll have to go at it carefully. Nail him so smoothly he'll never know what hit him. I mean, why make the guy gun-shy?"

I found my breath. "But Mary Alice, I *can't* —"

"Just leave the details to me. I'll make all the arrangements. Subtleness counts. And we both know how subtle I can be."

I beat down the urge to laugh out loud.

"First of all, I'll sound Bob out. Which means check on what else he does besides play sandlot baseball. And if the check comes up positive, I'll round up Don and set up another double date.

After which —" She stopped short, her eyebrows flying up to meet her hairline. "Oh, good grief, guess who's coming across your front lawn?"

I debated the wisdom of guessing who.

"Well!" Mary Alice hopped up from the glider. "Darned if I'll stay around here and listen to Jeremy Barnes take over our conversation!" And off she ran, with a speed I wouldn't have believed possible, zipping past Jeremy with her nose in the air.

I took her place on the glider, inching over to give Jeremy a spot to sit on. Assuming, that is, he'd want to sit.

I might have guessed he wouldn't. And I might have expected the bruised tone of voice coming past his accusing face.

"Think you're pretty cute, don't you?"

I hunched my shoulders and tried a smile. "Well . . ."

"Walking out like that," he fumed. "Leaving us flat. Boy, did the guys ask questions!" His voice rose and cracked. "And what was I supposed to tell them? You'd developed a concussion, or maybe sudden amnesia, and wandered off?"

Giving me the germ of an idea. I put a hand to my forehead and sort of moaned, thinking to fake a head injury. But Jeremy had spent years seeing past my fakes. He wasn't buying now.

"You don't plan on coming back, do you?"

I stared mutely up at him.

"What's the *matter* with you, Red?" He asked that quietly enough. But I could feel the rush of some kind of emotion behind his words. As if, inside him, all sorts of private wars were going on. "Since when have you turned quitter?"

I bit back some words of my own. Jeremy had scratched a surface wound and left it bleeding. I'd always been so proud of my ability to stick with a thing until it died of old age.

"Well?" Jeremy scowled at me. "Cat got your tongue?"

Okay, if that was the way he wanted to play. "About sandlot ball," I said. "It's just not enough for me anymore."

"What do you *mean*, not enough? After all the hours of practice, all the figuring of strategy to turn you into a first-rate shortstop, you're telling me —"

"Oh, sure, I'll admit I was pretty hung up on the shortstop thing. For a while. But, Jeremy, goals do change. Kids grow up. There's a big old world out there, just waiting to be lived in. And I —"

"Don't know what's happened to my ears. I could have sworn I just heard —"

"And, as Mary Alice says, socially I'm way back there with the little kids. Which means it's about time I —"

"*Mary Alice*," Jeremy shouted. "I might have guessed!"

The dotted swiss curtains in the living room window suddenly twitched, and my mother's face peered out. She rapped on a windowpane. I could see her lips form words: "What's going on out there?"

Jeremy must have caught it, too. The tips of

his ears flamed scarlet, and he backed away from me. But he was still plenty wound up. "All right, you just play the prima donna!" He glared at me. "We have us one Gopher who wants to play that spot so bad he can taste it. Bob Murray."

Did my face change expression? Jeremy eyed me, frowning as if trying to figure something out. "Well, I don't know what's so ha-ha about Bob Murray taking over as shortstop. He's a *real* pro. None of that walk-out stuff from old Bob. When you left, you probably did him the favor of the year. In fact," he added, laying it on, "some of the guys might even think you did the whole team a favor."

"Ouch," I said softly.

Anger drained from Jeremy's face. He edged the tip of his right sneaker along a porch floorboard. "I didn't mean that, Red," he said. "The guys don't really feel that way at all. Not even Bob Murray."

I let my breath out carefully, hoping to reduce the almost overwhelming urge to burst into tears.

"Can I at least tell the guys you're thinking it over and might change your mind?" he asked, looking hopeful.

There was this silence, while Jeremy and I stared at each other. Then I shook my head.

"Well, in that case . . ." Jeremy hesitated. And then, "See ya, Red," he said. He turned, clumped down the porch steps and, without looking back, loped across the street to his house.

He phoned later. We talked in a normal, friendly way for maybe fifteen minutes, about this and that. He said he'd stop by in the morning to walk me to school, I said, "Fine with me, Jeremy," and we hung up.

Mary Alice called just before ten. Thank heavens my mother got to the phone first. Mary Alice's voice carries something awful. I could hear her through the phone line, clear into the living room, where I was huddled in front of the TV, trying to escape All. Somehow, the thought of having to gab with Mary Alice (which would mean listening to her rehash the whole dreary day, then volunteer her opinion, and suggest what I should and shouldn't do about subjects I preferred not to discuss) left me cold. So when Mom mouthed, "It's for you, Jody," I shook my head at her and returned to the TV.

"I, uh, believe she's gone to bed, Mary Alice," Mom said, not looking the least uncomfortable as she lied. I think my mother figured lying to Mary Alice Martinson wouldn't be classed as the worst thing she'd ever do in this life.

She didn't even bother to cross-examine me about it, the way she sometimes does. In fact, Mom's only response was a mild, "Jody, next time that girl calls, make sure you're really somewhere else, so you don't put me on the spot like that." And she was smiling when she said it.

Was it possible my mother understood, at least as well as I did, that a full dose of Mary Alice Martinson could be an overdose? Hey, a new thought. Was it also possible my mother understood *several* unsuspected things?

I didn't know. But one of these days I'd work on it.

SEVEN

Morning sun slanting off bedroom window blinds and flicking across my semiclosed eyelids brought me groggily to another day's life.

I yawned, stretched, and sat up, trying to work past the mental fog. My way is to struggle to the window, shove it up, and glance out. I recouped fast. My brain automatically recorded all that sunshine and checked out the temp. And telegraphed only good news.

A warm, sunny day would be right up my alley. A full afternoon's practice at the sandlot. Down to business on the double play, muscling up for batting practice, and —

And then I *really* woke up.

So who needed sun? Slamming down the window, I inched over to the dresser mirror and glared into it. I groaned from the depths of my soul and scurried away as if chased. Then I made it back to bed, where I slumped on the edge and contemplated my next move (if any).

I figured *forget it*, slid underneath the covers, yanked them up to my chin, and closed my eyes.

Well, maybe I could do something about my hair. Comb it, anyway. And try out that expensive-looking face cream I'd sneaked from my mother's store of bottles, tubes, and jars. White stuff with deep-cleaning action guaranteed to lift out epidermal impurities.

I sat up on one elbow, still thinking, and remembered, for one thing, the royal blue turtleneck sweater my Aunt Rose from Sacramento had sent the Christmas before. Would it go with the navy pants Mom had given me on my fourteenth birthday (which I'd shoved, still in the package, into my bottom drawer)?

Not that it really mattered.

But just in case it did, I laid the knitted top and pants across my bed, grabbed up the face cream, and padded down the hall to the bathroom.

Where, wouldn't you know it, Mike had made it ahead of me. That boy certainly could hog time and space. I heard him flipping the pages of a magazine and humming to himself, as if he had all the time in the world. But over the years I'd developed techniques for luring him out.

"What d'you *mean*, Gail is downstairs looking for me?" he squawked, stepping this side of the bathroom door with a towel draped (barely) around his lower half. Then he caught on. Too late. I'd already zipped past him and safely locked the door.

So it took me a while. I don't know why he figured pounding on the door and hollering after my first fifteen minutes in there would change anything, but that's my beloved brother Mike for you. Impatient, inconsiderate . . .

I try to ignore unfriendly comments. At the breakfast table that morning they came swift and fast. Everybody seemed infected by sourness. Like one big growl. It was almost a relief to hear Jeremy's familiar rat-a-tat on our front door.

Thank heavens Jeremy was acting his UN Delegate best, gabbing with my father, listening carefully while Mom sounded off about her picky little peeves, even smoothing Mike's ruffled feathers with a word dropped here and there. As I say, at that particular moment he was operating at his best.

As the air mellowed, Jeremy gathered up my books, flashed his "let's go" grin, and off we went.

For a block and a half, nothing of interest (except Jeremy's line of chatter) went on. And I followed his bright sounds as I often have. With enjoyment. He sidestepped any mention of the Gophers and their future plans, making absolutely no effort to pressure me. Nobody can call Jeremy Barnes a dummy. I mean, if ever there were a way to lure me back to the sandlot, that psychology should have done it. And nine times out of ten, Jeremy's shrewd moves pay off.

"Hey," I cut in suddenly, poking his arm to draw attention. "Over there on the sidewalk. With the green scarf. It's —"

"Mary Alice." The corners of Jeremy's mouth flattened out. "Naturally. She would turn up. Bad pennies usually do."

"Oh, she's" — I shrugged — "okay." And then, on impulse, "Jeremy, let's catch up with her."

"No!" Jeremy dug in his heels, refusing to budge. "Listen, I'm as democratic as the next guy. But I draw the line at —"

"Chicken," I muttered, moving forward. Mary Alice obviously wasn't about to wait up for me. She'd spotted Bob Murray loping along ahead of us all. I could tell by the jut of her shoulders and the clack-clack of her pace, she'd overtake him or die trying. And I figured I knew why.

"Oh, brother," Jeremy said, whacking his forehead, "now she thinks she'll latch onto old Bob!" The gleeful expression on his face plainly said, "Boy, is she due for a shock!"

"Hey, *Roberto*," Mary Alice shrieked, waving her arms as she broke into a run, "wait for me!"

Bob clumped to a halt and glanced over his shoulder. He scowled and I guess would have hurried on, except Mary Alice had already caught up to him and cornered him.

"Now, you just watch," Jeremy instructed. "She'll try to get him to listen, and he'll give her the cold shoulder. Then she'll . . ." His voice trailed off as Bob and Mary Alice stood there with their heads together, talking in low tones.

"So, I'm watching," I said, concentrating on the scene before us. "But for a guy about to give the cold shoulder, I'd say he looks pret-ty cozy."

"I just don't get it," Jeremy said, rubbing at his chin. "I know for a fact Murray can't stand that barracuda. So why he's wasting his time on —"

"Oh, look," I said, pointing. "There they go down the street. Together. And I must say he seems to be hanging onto her every word."

"What could those two possibly have to rap about?" Jeremy wanted to know. "They have nothing in common. He's gung-ho about sports, and she's gung-ho about Don Petrie. He hates anyone bossy like poison. She considers all us Gophers a bunch of juveniles. So I can't understand why . . ."

Jeremy worried that bone all the way to school. I sort of listened, but most of my thoughts were wandering up there with Mary Alice and Bob. What honeyed words was she pouring into his ears? Miracle words? Because it would take a miracle to jar the Reluctant Wonder into action. And action was what Mary Alice had in mind.

What was I letting myself in for this time? Why couldn't I be satisfied with —

"You've heard my side of it, Red. Now, what's your opinion?"

I wheeled around. "Uh . . ." I caught Jeremy's eye. "Absolutely, Jeremy," I said, bobbing my head. "I agree wholeheartedly with everything you said." Which should cover all bases.

"Very interesting," he said, a tiny smile crinkling his lips. "First time you ever agreed with me on *that* subject."

I opened my mouth, thought better of it, closed my mouth. The story of my life, these days. Caught with my foot off first base.

Jeremy and I got together at noon in the cafeteria, over hot roast-beef sandwiches. He was still stewing about Mary Alice. "Would you believe," he mumbled past a hunk of roast beef, "she actually had him trapped in Algebra, where she wasn't even supposed to *be*, for pete's sake! Might just as well have grabbed Bob by the ear and hung on, the way she was running at the mouth. And she was telling him —"

"Oh?" Delicately I picked a shred of green vegetation from what the cafeteria staff laughingly called a tossed salad. "You, uh, heard what they were discussing?"

He gave up chomping and swallowed the beef semiwhole. "Well, not exactly. I leaned their way with both ears flapping. But Mr. Elwood made some crack about kids who didn't belong in Algebra taking up valuable time, and he gave her his cold-fish eye, so she backed off. But Mary Alice is up to something, mark my words. And when I find out —"

I dropped the vegetation. "Ughh," I said, wrinkling my nose. "I know the staff means well, but . . ."

"Do what I do," Jeremy advised. "Drown the stuff in French dressing. By the time you make it to the rest of the ingredients, the tossed salad's halfway down your gullet."

It had possibilities. But since the nearest bottle of French dressing was two tables to our left, and *Bob Murray* was two tables to our left, maybe I wouldn't.

"Matter of fact," Jeremy went on, "I'd try out my own brilliant solution if only we had us some French dressing. I wonder where —"

"I see some!" I hopped up, meaning to grab the French dressing out from under Bob's nose and return to the safety of good old Jeremy.

What happened was I stuck out my hand to

grab it, and Bob Murray did some grabbing of his own, catching my right hand in both of his and jiggling it like a pump handle. "Well, well," he said, "if it isn't my ex-teammate!"

I wracked what was left of my brain, trying to ferret out something bright and clever to snap back with.

"Awful rough paw for a girl," Bob said. He turned my palm up and critically eyed the callus along the inside of my thumb. "Whatever happened to those golden days of yore, when a girl's hand felt like a girl's hand?"

I could have countered with what rough old mitts *boys* had, only I didn't trust the sound of my own voice. And this funny tingle had started in my palm and was traveling rapidly up my arm, practically paralyzing it from the elbow down. Which pretty much ruled out yanking my hand away.

Bob was staring at me with these glittery eyes, as if he could read my mind, right down to the last comma.

"I, uh, just came over to get the, uh, Fr . . . Fr . . ." What was happening to me? I sounded as if I had a mouthful of marbles! Stupid? I couldn't remember when I'd felt more stupid.

"Hey, Red!" From Jeremy, who was standing up now, trying to see past two other kids' heads and a moving food tray. "Whatcha doing? *Making* that French dressing?"

Bob let go of my fingers, lowering my hand to the table and giving it a little pat. "Don't want to keep him waiting," he said, grinning. He held out the dressing. "See you later, Jo-dy."

Drawing my name out like a bow humming over a fiddle string.

"You sure took your sweet time," Jeremy let me know, reaching up and taking the bottle, then dolloping the stuff over his greens.

I, in the meantime, managed to sit down and perform a few other robotlike motions until Jeremy glanced over. He frowned. "What's the matter, Red? You look peculiar."

"Me? Pe-cu-liar?" I cleared my throat, trying to remove the squeak. "What do you mean?"

"Not only do you sound odd," he said, "but your face is red as a beet. I know it's warm in here, but —" His gaze wandered to the tables to our left. "Might have guessed," he said. "Bob Murray. That guy been needling you? I'll have to speak to him."

"I'd rather you didn't," I said in a strangled voice. And then, while the inside of me lapsed into this sort of coma, I became very animated on the outside. I ate my tossed salad with gusto and changed the subject at least six times. I laughed over dinky little nothings and breathed a sigh of relief when the bell rang.

Then I managed, somehow, to make it through the afternoon classes.

On the way home from school, Jeremy tried a new tack. "Okay, so you want off the team," he said. "But nothing says you can't *watch*, right? Listen, the Gophers will need all the backing they can get! So why don't I save room for you on the bench? You can maybe work on the lineups, keep score when we start the games."

Yeah. And watch Bob Murray shine in my old

spot between second and third or agonize while they broke in a new Gopher, some kid who wanted to play so bad, he'd work *any* position just to be part of the team.

"I have in mind a sort of assistant manager," Jeremy said, enlarging on his idea. "You and me running the team, making the crucial moves. But no decisions now, Red." He cut himself short. "You go home and think about it."

Most of the afternoon I stuck like glue to the porch glider, creaking back and forth as if my life depended on it, until my mother, up to her ears in creaks, hollered past the screen door for me to quit. So I just sat like a lump, observing the Arbutus Street comings and goings. Big deal. Between three and four, I counted six cars going north, and five cars and a truck going south. The Lassiter twins, who live next door, fought over volleyball on their side lawn. Jeremy's sister Victoria was necking with her guy on the Barnes front steps, apparently not caring that half the world could see them there. Three dogs had chased the Roberts cat up a tree and were yapping their heads off. Now and then I'd peek at my wristwatch, then glance up Arbutus, looking for some sign of Jeremy.

Mom likes to say that lack of action is bad for the soul. I don't know how it affects other people's souls, but it sure wasn't doing much for mine. After a while I hauled myself up and wandered out to the garage where I looked up my old tennis racket and a ball. I bounced some experimental shots off the garage wall. Then I checked my watch again. By now sandlot practice should definitely be over. Where *was* Jeremy? I slammed a vicious shot against the wall. And another. And another.

I don't know how long he'd been part of the scene. Bob Murray, I mean. But there he was, occupying space on our back lawn, watching me lay it on that ball.

"Good to see you're keeping in shape," he said.

My face flamed hot. I took a quick swipe at the ball and missed.

"Of course, you are a little out of practice."

I figured I had to be losing my touch. All the biting remarks I could have snapped back didn't even make it to my mouth.

"What I came over here for," Bob said, scuffing the toe of one outsized gym shoe along our patio flagstones, "is, well, Mary Alice sort of clued me in on . . . *you* know. Why you gave up your big chance at shortstop. And I gotta tell you, Red, that was the most *unselfish* —"

One more swipe sent the ball a little high, barely clearing the garage window.

"And then, when Jeremy told me you wanted out of the Gophers, I almost swallowed my eye-teeth! Oh, not that I blame you," he added quickly. "I mean, you *are* a girl, Red. And trading baseball tips with a bunch of guys must get pretty boring. But I do feel like maybe I've *pushed* you."

I collared the tennis ball and threw it hard against the garage wall, caught it, and threw it again.

"What I have in mind," Bob slipped in between all this, "is maybe you and me sitting down and . . . *hey*, Red, will you quit that for a sec?"

Well, okay, I'd sit. Bob found a spot near the flowering crab apple tree, and I plunked myself down next to the birdbath. He moved closer, and I backed up just a little. That seemed to do it.

"The way I see it," Bob said, stretching his legs out among the dandelions and resting the back of his head against the birdbath pedestal, "you did me a favor, so I owe you one. Like Mary Alice says, a guy has to sacrifice now and then. So, I'm taking you out."

I waited for this stupid fluttering in my chest to die down. "You call that a favor, Murray?" I split a blade of grass and stuck it in my mouth. "Who needs it?"

"Now wait," he said, sitting up. "I guess I put that sort of funny. What I meant was, I'd *like* to take you out. I mean, I'm *asking* you, Red. Will you go out with me?"

Well, put *that* way . . . *hmmm.*

"I figure we could make it a foursome. You and me, Mary Alice and Don. How about the amusement park in Fleet City, for starters? Mary Alice says Don can get free tickets for some of the rides, and I've saved a little money from my morning paper route, so what do you say?"

I shrugged. "Oh, I guess."

"Good," Bob said, scrambling to his feet and actually looking pleased. "Then we'll — oh, *hi*, Jeremy!"

Yes, Jeremy. Standing perfectly still, a few feet from us, his face wiped of expression.

Should I have said something? I've never been great at that sort of skill. Besides, it's a little difficult trying to converse with somebody who all of a sudden hauls around and walks away from you. Unless you don't mind totally embarrassing yourself by hollering explanations to a rapidly retreating back. . . .

EIGHT

"Okay, *okay*," Jeremy croaked through the phone line, "so I won't let it bother me. I mean, why should *I* care if Bob Murray wants to drag you to some crummy old amusement park and blow a few bucks on a bunch of sappy rides and hot dogs and cotton candy? Why should I get all upset?"

His voice had risen to a high note and cracked. Jeremy was bothered, all right. "It's not like it sounds." I tried to explain. "What happened was, Don Petrie had these free tickets, see? And he and Mary Alice were going, and she thought it would be more fun if another couple came along, so she thought of Bob . . . and me. Naturally I'd be a dope to turn down a freebie."

"Naturally," Jeremy said.

Pause. "Hey, Jeremy, I've got a super idea! Why don't we make it a fivesome? You and me and Bob, and Mary Alice and —"

"No *way*!"

"Now hold it, Jeremy Barnes," I said, doing an about-face. "If Bob Murray wants to take me out, what's the crime? And speaking of big spenders, can you remember the last time you broke down and treated me to something more exciting than a candy bar?"

You could almost reach out and touch the silence at the other end of the line.

"Jeremy?"

"I suppose if I got *me* a morning paper route . . ."

Jeremy really knew how to zing in the old guilt. "It's not the money, you knucklehead! What I'm talking about is, well, going someplace *special*. Like *couples* do. But since you never ask me —"

"I could do yard work for the Markhams. Or fill in down at the discount store. Maybe stock their shelves. Or check out the Longworths on Lincoln Avenue. That mammoth lawn —"

"Jeremy, are you *listening* to me?"

Pregnant pause. And then, "Hey, Red, I'll catch you in the A.M., okay? Got a little heavy thinking to do."

"Jere-*mee*!"

Dead line.

A pretty unsatisfactory phone conversation all the way around.

We planned the date for Saturday afternoon — after Gopher practice, but early enough so that Don (who had to argue, this time, to get the use of his father's car) could get us home before dark.

You might say Jeremy and I discussed it

further on the way to school. If you consider short bursts of speech from me, punctuated by gruff "Okay, *okay*"s from Jeremy, followed by a rapid, walking-away stride (forcing me to catch up with him and try again), discussing. A little bit of this goes a long way. So I quit discussing, and Jeremy slowed down for me, and we trudged to school more or less in silence.

He opened my locker for me. I lent him my extra blue pen. We arranged to split cafeteria rations during our lunch break. So it went. To the half-blind observer, things may have looked and sounded pretty much as always.

Jeremy was hanging around his front lawn, leaning on a hoe handle that Saturday afternoon when Don and Mary Alice drove in. He waved briefly to Don and glared at Mary Alice (who ignored him, out of habit). But when Bob Murray sauntered into view, he suddenly became busy, ferociously attacking sections of grass, yanking out large tufts of it with the hoe and tossing them into a pile. I was sure his father would have a fit. Who wouldn't, after seeing those unsightly clumps of sod junked along his driveway?

Mary Alice had suggested dressing for comfort. I'd pondered that one for a while. Comfort, to me, had always been patched jeans and any old sweat shirt. But I could see (in my mind's eye) Bob staring at my idea of easy-does-it, then arching his brows and giving some acid comment. So I dressed carefully in a pantsuit I'd worn just once. And I worked a long time over my face — foundation cream, touches of eye shadow and mascara, eyeliner, blusher, all the other stuff. The whole tedious bit. The Mount Vesuvius had shriveled to a mere dot, easily hidden with the medicated glop. And I tried something different with my hair — a half-bang casually brushing my right eye and soft curls tickling the lobes of my ears. The mirror told me I looked not too bad.

Bob's eyes told me the same thing. And as we eased into the backseat of Don's father's car, they were still on me. I could see his lips move, as if working on a message of some kind. But when I smiled at him, he sort of shrank back against the seat and, I swear, blushed.

It really seemed as if things might be looking up for a change. Which only proves how much I had to learn.

One thing about Bob Murray, he certainly wasn't large on small talk. "Yups" and "nopes" wear a little thin after the first few minutes. For a time back there, I found myself longing for Jeremy's cheerful voice spouting his endless batting statistics and bits of trivia. But then I sneaked a glance at Bob's profile as he peered through the car window, and the longing fled.

A very good-looking guy, Mary Alice had called him. No argument from me on that. I *liked* the way his face was put together — that gorgeous nose, the shag of honey-blond hair, those deep blue eyes.

Bob turned from the window and stared at me. He mumbled something. And a hammer pounded inside my chest. Was I supposed to return a mumble with a mumble? I looked quickly away, my throat feeling as if it were filled with cotton fluff.

"Hey, there," Mary Alice called out from the front seat. "What's going on, you two?"

Bob grabbed hold of my hand (accidentally bending one finger sideways, not that I was about to tell him). "Oh, wouldn't you like to know!" He flashed me a grin, as if we were sharing a private joke. And then he released my hand and went back to staring out the window. But the damage had been done. My pulsebeat would never be the same.

While the guys bought our entrance tickets, Mary Alice and I stood on the sidelines waiting. More exactly, I was waiting, and she was talking. Spilling in my ear a slew of tips on how to handle Bob Murray. "And remember," she cautioned, "play it female. Let *him* be the strong, masterly one, guiding poor, weak little you into safe paths of . . . oh, hi, boys! All set? Let's go!"

What I *wanted* to tell her was how truly dumb I thought the idea was. I'd been me all of my life. Why should I suddenly turn into that strange, hypocritical creature Mary Alice had so lovingly labeled "female"? But she seemed to have so many answers. . . .

Hey, I *tried*. Nobody can say I didn't. Still, what did Mary Alice really expect? This leopard to change her spots?

I started off well. I did all the so-called right things when we climbed into that roller coaster —clung to Bob when we began each mile-high trek upward, shrieked as if in mortal terror when we zoomed bottomward, let him help poor, weak little me out of the coaster car, and tottered to the next ride under protest, finally allowing Bob to talk me into it, sticking to him like glue all the way.

And then somebody got the brilliant idea to try the rifle range.

Bob asked me if I'd ever done any. Target-shooting, I mean. I was about to tell the truth when I caught Mary Alice violently shaking her head. "Uh, no, never," I lied. Mary Alice nodded her approval.

Bob showed me how to hold the rifle, how to sight in the target, the correct way to squeeze the trigger. I tried to look as much of a novice as possible. Jeremy would really have flipped over my act. He'd have known, better than anyone, how accurate I could be. We'd learned the skill together. Just the two of us, under my dad's supervision. And I could beat Jeremy eight times out of ten.

"My ma always says ladies first," Bob said, showing all his pearly teeth as he handed me a rifle. Gorgeous though his incisors might be without the braces, I didn't quite buy that smile. Did he want me to flunk out? Was it possible that, even here, on this penny ante rifle range, Murray couldn't bear to have me outdo him? Well, we'd soon find out! I'd show *him* —

"Remember," Mary Alice whispered from her post behind me, "*he's* the winner. Because if he wins, *you* win. Get me?"

I barely heard her.

I zeroed in on those little pasteboard ducks bobbing along on their track. My trigger finger settled into place. And then Mary Alice's words sank in, and I eased the sight up and to the right, and squeezed.

"Boy, are you ever a rotten shot," Bob chortled. "I could do better with my eyes closed!"

I pasted on a sickly grin. But inside me, nothing was grinning.

Bob bought himself five rounds. He got two, nicked one duck without downing it, missed two cleanly. Nothing spectacular, but he looked pretty satisfied with himself. "Okay, Jody," he said, shelling out for five shots for me. "Here's your big chance to prove I was right about girls all along!"

That did it.

This time, looking past Mary Alice's watchful face, I sighted in carefully and squeezed the trigger. Pasteboard splattered in several directions.

"Beginner's luck," Bob muttered to nobody in particular. "Any dummy could —"

Pow! Splat.

"Hey, wow," Don Petrie said and whistled low. From Bob, nothing.

I squeezed and caught the next duck square, sending it to pasteboard heaven.

Mary Alice was disapproving like mad behind me. I could almost feel her face freeze. But Don was leaning forward, alive with interest. "I think we have a winner here," he piped up. "Anybody want to place a bet?" From Bob, a sort of snort.

How can I explain my reaction to that? Maybe there is no explanation for a competitive hardhead with victory breathing down her neck. I picked up the rifle, loaded it, drew a bead on my target, blasted away, and watched the duck disintegrate. I reloaded, drew another bead, blasted, and watched. A perfect score. I set the rifle down, turned, and permitted myself a tiny smile. "So, who's next?"

"Not me," said Don, shaking his head. "Don't know how you did that, Jody, but you sure oughta patent it."

If looks could kill, Mary Alice's would have annihilated Don. She sashayed over to where Bob was huddled, fists jammed in pockets, lower lip stuck out a mile. "Come on, Robert," she said, grabbing his arm and yanking him toward her. "Let's go. I feel the urgent need for some refreshment."

Which naturally left Don and me standing there looking pretty extra. They practically ran all the way to the nearest refreshment stand. From a distance we watched Bob lean over to Mary Alice and whisper something. She glanced up at him and giggled. Then she said something that produced three hot dogs for him and a giant-sized strawberry malted for her. And as we watched, Mary Alice selected two straws from a pile of them, handed one to Bob, then dipped the other into the malted.

I inched to within hearing distance. Just in time to catch Mary Alice's businesslike slurp. Then Bob, bringing his face close to hers, stuck his straw into the malted. And the two of them slurped away, until all that was left was a trickle of strawberry melted that had dripped onto the counter top. But their faces stayed over the empty cup — just hanging there, frozen in fuzzy silence.

"Hey," Don yelped, moving closer. "Hey, what's going *on* here?"

"Nothing that would interest *you*," Mary Alice snapped, scalding him with a look.

Bob was too busy munching on a hot dog to say anything. I tried to catch his eye. But no go.

"Not to change the subject," Don said, "but we did come here to have some fun. And right now I can't say I'm —"

"Roberto," Mary Alice cut in, waving her straw under Bob's nose, "what say you and I take in the local sights?"

"Why not?" Bob got to his feet. "Which way?"

Mary Alice stared at him through half-closed lids. "Well, I have this particular place in mind."

Would you believe Bob Murray actually left behind half his hot dog just to follow her?

Of course, he did turn around with a smirk to mutter, "See you guys later." For which Don and I were supposed to be eternally grateful?

Don looked as if somebody'd just cracked him over the head with a croquet mallet. He'd probably be rooted there yet, if I hadn't spotted this bench nearby and sort of guided him to it. He sat down heavily and rested his elbows on his knees. Then he cupped his chin in his palm and gazed into the far-off.

Total silence tends to unnerve me, so I cleared my throat, all set to make some bright comment. But just then —

"I don't get it," Don said. "I do *not* get it!"

"Uh," I contributed.

"You take a girl here and there for six months, she accepts your friendship ring, she makes big noises about going steady, then some other guy comes along, and *poof!*"

"*Poof,*" I echoed feelingly. I caught Don's eye and sighed. He slid over, making room for me. And there we sat. Like two lumps.

"On the other hand," Don said after a while, "maybe we're overreacting. So they split a malted and took off along the boardwalk for a change of scenery. Is that a catastrophe?"

"You're right, of course," I said, sitting up straight. "I mean, I know for a fact Bob positively doesn't go for Mary Alice. He considers her bossy and irritating."

"Well, he's not exactly Sir Galahad himself," Don cut in, darting me a sharp look. He stood up and glanced hopefully around. "For one thing, Mary Alice has always been attracted to older guys. Like me." He loped off in the general direction of the boardwalk, talking over his shoulder. "And you *know* what she thinks of those screwy Gophers."

"Right," I said, hurrying to catch up with him. "Nothing could possibly be happening. She's probably just trying to get you jealous, and Bob's nose is out of joint because I showed him up on the rifle range."

But suddenly there they were, on their own private bench, a few yards from the boardwalk. Bob's right hand was clutching the remains of a candied apple, and Mary Alice had an empty container of popcorn. Bob's hair was rumpled, as if somebody had run wild fingers through it. And his eyes were glazed. I could tell that all the way from where Don and I were standing with our eyes attached to the sight. And as we watched, some candy from the apple got stuck in Mary Alice's hair when Bob leaned forward to kiss her.

A messy scene in more ways than one.

We made it back to Don's father's car without bloodshed. But not before a number of words had blued the air. The kind that you wish later you could take back. Lucky for me, most of them were Don's.

It certainly didn't do much for the ride home. Mary Alice was still up front with Don. But not *with* Don, if you know what I mean. Bob was no longer staring out of the window. His gaze was now riveted on the back of Mary Alice's head. And he had this absolutely *soupy* expression on his face. As if he were about to drown in his own emotions.

I sat as far away from Bob as I could get. For some reason it seemed important not to touch him or even speak to him. Otherwise, the inside of me felt numb — as if I'd been stabbed, but the pain hadn't surfaced yet.

Who'd have believed a thirty-mile ride home from Fleet City could take so long?

Don slowed the car at our driveway. I opened the door and got out.

Which apparently brought Bob Murray back to life. "Hey, wait, Jody," he hollered. "I'll walk you to your door!"

I didn't bother to turn around. "Thanks, but

no thanks," I said, my voice like sandpaper in my throat. And I marched up the front walk.

Behind me I could hear voices. Loud ones, coming from the car. Don's baritone sounded over all, and then I heard Mary Alice's answering snap, as only Mary Alice can snap. And Bob's plaintive croak from the backseat.

I turned just in time to see Don's father's car lurch forward as if tiny devils had taken charge of the engine. Bob's head jerked likewise, and Mary Alice's arm moved, connecting with some part of Don's anatomy. I'll never know which part because the next thing I saw they were rattling up Arbutus, trailed by little clouds of exhaust.

It hit me as I reached the top porch step. And, *wow*, did it hurt! Suddenly I'd become all rubbery legs, barely able to totter over to the glider and plunk myself into it.

But how long could I creak there without bringing the rest of the family out? They'd see me *bawling*. And, yeah, there'd be questions. Stupid, embarrassing questions.

After a panicky minute, my eyes focused on the Barnes house. But Jeremy was nowhere in sight. Only those clods of front lawn uglying up the edges of their driveway showed where he'd been.

So okay, he was probably in the house, sprawled as usual in front of the TV, munching on some M & M's, taking in the final innings of the Saturday afternoon baseball game.

I knew I had to talk my mixed-up feeling out

with someone. And suddenly, nobody but Jeremy would do.

Mrs. Barnes came to their front door. "Jeremy?" she repeated. "Why, he's . . . *Victoria*," she yelled, "where did Jeremy say he was going?"

I could see Victoria making some kind of scene with her guy Jack in the den just off their entry hall. "He went to the Longworths'," she hollered back. "On some special project is what he said. Whatever *that* means."

Mr. and Mrs. Longworth lived in this big, old brick house on Lincoln Avenue, circled by plenty of lawn and several flower borders. They had three daughters. Blondes.

"Why don't you come in and wait for him?" Mrs. Barnes volunteered. "He shouldn't be much longer. It's almost dinnertime. And you know how Jeremy is when it comes to eating."

So I'd wait. For a while. Not comfortably, because Victoria and her guy insisted on wandering into the living room (where I was trying to concentrate on the eleventh inning of a Giants-Mets game). How Jeremy could stand that kissing scene day after day I'd never know.

After a while Mrs. Barnes set the table and brought in the meat and vegetables, then invited me to eat with them. But I wasn't feeling especially hungry. I mean, without Jeremy there to kid around with . . .

"I can't understand what's taking that boy so long," Mrs. Barnes said, looking anxious. "It isn't like him to skip a meal."

Later, after she cleared the table, she called up the Longworths to find out why.

Jeremy, it turned out, had decided to eat with the Longworths. Why should *I* care that he didn't rush home when his mother told him I was there waiting?

I left while Mrs. Barnes was still on the phone, running through the small talk with a Longworth. She didn't glance up. Either she didn't hear me go or it didn't matter to her one way or the other.

Jeremy didn't get home until ten o'clock. I know that for a fact, because I was on our porch — in the dark — watching. I mean, I figured *somebody* had to watch out for Jeremy.

Although I will confess I didn't expect to hear him whistling so cheerfully as he loped up his front walk. And I did kind of hope he'd at least glance over our way and see me.

NINE

But nobody escapes me forever. I caught Jeremy the next morning, picking up those clumps of lawn and dropping them into a bushel basket.

"Your father sore about it?" I asked, grabbing up a clump and tossing it toward the basket, just to show whose side I was on.

"Sore? Why should he be sore?" Jeremy drop-kicked one in the general direction of the driveway. "He's *paying* me for doing it."

"Paying? Why would anybody in his right mind pay a person to dig holes in his lawn?"

"Landscaping, my friend. Landscaping." He waved a hand here and there. "You will note the spacing. Exactly five feet apart. Pop has big plans for our lawn. I'm laying out the area scientifically for him, and when he borrows back his spade from your dad, I'll —"

"Oh, sure! Next thing you'll tell me you've switched your career goals from computer science to landscaping. Become Jeremy Barnes, master landscaper. Come *on*."

"Sneer all you want." Jeremy hauled some dead tree branches from the lawn. "It's healthy, honest work, and it pays."

"Of course, if you have to depend on your *father* . . ."

He broke the branches down to basket-size. "Yeah, and the Longworths. And anybody else I can scare up."

"But that'll leave you next to no time —"

"Right." Jeremy snapped a branch into several pieces and pitched them into the basket. "But now and then one must look beyond the immediate moment. One must learn to sacrifice the good times for the old payola." He eyed me. "Am I making my point?"

What did he expect me to say? Let's hope nothing. Because that's what I said.

"Oh, by the way, Red," Jeremy added, picking up the basket, "I won't be able to walk to school with you mornings. At least, not for a few weeks. Mr. Longworth's lined up these chores for me, see? I'll have to be up at six sharp, beat it over there, work like a steam engine, run back home, wash up, and jump into my school clothes. You do understand, don't you?"

"But the afternoons —"

"They'll pretty much be taken up with Gopher practice. I'll *try* to arrange my schedule so we can walk home together." Jeremy shrugged. Then he retreated up the driveway. "See ya around, Red."

It wasn't until later, after I'd wandered back

to my own house, that I remembered. I'd forgotten all about telling Jeremy what had gone wrong back there at the amusement park.

My brother Mike *would* have to notice it first.

Mike jogs. He liked to think he was what held together the Wilmont High track team last spring. Any morning at five-thirty would find him in his orange-and-brown track suit, pounding along Arbutus, down Woodward Avenue, up Main, onto Lincoln Avenue, and back onto Arbutus. Rotten timing brought him into contact with Jeremy, who was slipping along the back fences leading to the Longworths. And pure nosiness slowed him down to watch.

"I wouldn't have believed the kid could hustle like that," he marveled at the breakfast table. "Longworth really had him moving his tail. Although I'll bet that cute little blonde hanging around out there didn't exactly cramp Jeremy's style."

I did a quick mental rundown of which of the three Longworth daughters would be most likely. And settled on Holly.

"Holly? Yeah, she's the one." Mike helped himself to a fourth slice of toast, laying on the butter with a heavy hand.

"She's just a *child*." I dismissed Holly as I drowned a chocolate chip cookie in a glass of milk.

"Is that right? Have you checked out that so-called child lately?" Mike whistled (one of those low, meaningful sounds guys use when . . . *you* know when), then grinned.

"So, who cares?" I tossed it off. "You know perfectly well Jeremy isn't into that sort of thing yet."

"Oh, no? Then I'd better send my eyes back for a repair job. He was looking pretty much into it from where I stood."

I ran out of words and appetite at the same time.

The easiest part was lugging my own books to school. The toughest had to be waking up in the morning knowing that, for me, it would be just another morning. Jeremy wouldn't be elbowing past our front door, hollering out a greeting, then flicking on the *Today* show, planting his size nines on Mom's hassock, his head against the chair cushion, digging into his precious M & M's and chewing absently while absorbing the details of the news and weather.

Oh, sure, we still met at the lockers before first period. We still split our lunches. And some afternoons we walked home from school together. But anyone could see that inside Jeremy Barnes's head, strange, new thoughts were brewing.

I suppose I could have bombarded him with a million questions. But sometimes, with Jeremy, you just wait awhile.

"About the Gophers," he said abruptly one afternoon before the first sandlot game. "We got this new guy in town, Al Marks, for center field. To fill in at Bob's old position." He glanced over at me. "But I'm keeping your name on the roster. Just in case you ever change your mind."

Part of me leaped at the possibility. "How's

Bob doing at shortstop?" I asked, keeping my voice casual.

"As long as he keeps his mind on the game and off Mary Alice while he's playing," Jeremy said, "I won't knock him."

"And the new guy?"

"Coming along very well." Jeremy kicked at a stone, making it fly. "But he's not you, Red. What more can I tell you?"

The truth was, I missed those crazy old Gophers like anything. So why couldn't I bring myself to give in? What stubborn streak in me kept turning thumbs down? I couldn't understand my reasoning at all. So I changed the subject. "How's your early morning job coming along?" I asked.

"Mr. Longworth seems satisfied," Jeremy acknowledged, trying to look modest.

"I hear you've been getting a little help from your, uh, friend," I couldn't resist adding.

He darted me a swift glance. "Friend?" The tips of his ears reddened. "Oh, you must mean . . ."

"Holly," I finished for him.

"Holly," Jeremy repeated after me, as if he enjoyed the taste of her name on his tongue.

"And does Holly . . . um . . . does she like . . ." I trailed off, not knowing how to ask the question.

Jeremy picked up a white pebble and heaved it skyward. He waited, caught the pebble, and stuck it in his pocket. "You could say she knows I'm around. That's about it."

I think he meant to smile. But a layer of

Jeremy was hurting. You didn't need a microscope to spot that.

I suppose we could have discussed it. Once I'd have jumped at the chance.

We walked along in silence until we reached the corner of Woodward and Arbutus. Then Jeremy slowed to a halt. "By the way," he said. "I should warn you, I guess. You'll be receiving an invitation to a wedding soon."

Wedding? I stared at him.

"My sister Victoria is marrying Jack. Isn't that a blast?"

"But — she's too *young*!"

"For what?" Jeremy asked, his face suddenly bland.

It took a minute. "Oh," was all I said. I mean, what else *could* a person say?

The wedding ceremony took place the Saturday before the first Gopher game.

Actually, we Shepards weren't invited, if you're thinking in terms of engraved invitations and that sort of stuff. Mrs. Barnes merely phoned my mother and some other neighbors (along with a few relatives), and we gathered on that rainy evening in the Barnes living room, where they had this short little deal before the fireplace mantel, followed by ice cream, cake, and punch.

I sat next to my parents and behind Jeremy. While we were waiting for the ceremony to begin, Mom whispered to Dad, "I'm glad they decided to do it this quiet way. It's in much better taste."

Then Dad whispered back, "Andy Barnes told

me the sooner the better. Another month would be an embarrassment to the whole family."

Mike, sitting on the other side of them, smirked as if he knew a few choice items himself. Ahead of me, Jeremy stiffened in his chair, and the back of his neck turned bright red. It was a relief when his Aunt Lillie went to the piano and started up the chords to "O Promise Me."

The bride looked almost doll-like and fragile in her pale blue knit dress. The groom didn't smile once. Not before the ceremony or after. Jack kept filling up on punch. I got the feeling somebody there had spiked his, because as the evening wore on, his speech got blurred and he turned real sarcastic, snipping at everyone.

Until that day, I'd always considered weddings the happiest time for a girl and her guy. And their families.

Jeremy kept himself aloof from the rest of us, hovering in the vicinity of the ice cream. I watched him pile his plate high with butter pecan and pistachio, then sit down carefully and make experimental stabs at it. I think he downed two spoonfuls. It wasn't at all like Jeremy to allow his ice cream to melt.

I stared longingly at the empty chair next to his, then thought, *Why not?* and took it on myself to plunk into it.

Jeremy smiled at me, this odd little smile that held more sadness than it did laughter. And he said softly, "Great wedding, isn't it?"

We sat there for a while quietly, while the voices babbled on around us. Then Jeremy looked over at me. "Hey, Red, remember that day you and I found the trilobite down by the fork?"

I nodded.

"Remember that old house foundation? And the egg salad sandwiches? And the hot chocolate?"

"Yeah. And you laid down your new jacket for us to sit on and we ate and talked . . ."

Jeremy dipped his spoon into the two flavors. "For some reason I can't figure out," he said, "that was a very special day. One of the nicest days I've ever spent." His mouth suddenly pinched in at the corners, and for a nutty instant I got the distinct impression he was about to cry. But then he said, "Red, why do I get the feeling we'll never see a day like that again?"

I worked on a positive answer. Apparently not in time. Jeremy stood up quickly, spilling some ice cream onto the dining room rug. But he didn't appear to notice. He was too busy walking — no, running — across the room, away from me, and up the Barnes stairway.

The so-called festivities broke up shortly after that.

I probably wouldn't have gone, if Jeremy hadn't brought the subject up. But the least I could do for Jeremy — or the other guys — was to look in on the Gophers' first home game.

Due to this and that (okay, call it deliberate stalling), I got to the sandlot a little late. Halfway through the second inning, in fact, just as the Gophers took to the field.

First games usually draw a pretty good crowd. I had to wriggle past half of Arbutus Street, plus stragglers from out of the area, to get a decent view. And wouldn't you know, the only available spot would be a few paces away from Mary Alice Martinson?

I wasn't sure she'd even seen me. Still, who wanted to take the chance? Mary Alice had been on my blacklist ever since you know when. And eye to eye contact was the last thing I had in mind. But I needn't have worried. Her gaze was focused on only one person. Ye olde Gopher shortstop.

I must admit Bob Murray looked very okay out there — so absolutely pleased with himself, so at home in his spot between second and third.

I veered my gaze away from Mr. Wonderful and beaded in on the new kid in center field. Al Marks. Hmmm. At least he looked eager. As if he *wanted* to do his best. But Dave Lansing, the starting pitcher, appeared a bit shaky to me. The first batter up lucked out when Dave streaked a couple of balls down to Benny Armand that had to be called wild. And through some unnecessary fumbling, he got on base. He stole second with no trouble and kept eyeing third, just waiting for a slip in the command. Which made me uneasy. Because Joey Michaels, who occupied third, had developed a case of the wanders, as if meaning to cover a ten-block area with his one lonesome glove.

This obviously unsettled Jeremy. I watched him pace before the dugout, hands clasped behind his back, furrows crinkling his normally smooth forehead. He glanced out toward me. Then he went back to his pacing.

So why should all this make me feel so guilty, as if by quitting I had somehow set the whole team off balance? Should I go over to Jeremy and stick my nose in? Maybe second-guess as assistant manager, like he'd asked me to? Or should I just stand there, wringing my hands, feeling like the rat who'd deserted the sinking ship?

I watched, with growing horror, as the next batter up connected with a fair ball. And then, as if somebody'd finally pulled the right strings, the Gophers came to life. The batter had flied to center field. The new kid was on the ball like a hawk. He zinged it into third, where Joey magically appeared in the right place and caught it, tagging the sliding batter for the out. A perfectly executed double play.

I could see Jeremy unwind, then smile, as if a stroke of some master strategy had just paid off. And I knew, in that moment, the Gophers no more needed me than they needed an epidemic of measles.

By the end of the sixth inning the Gophers were ahead, fourteen to three. I didn't stick around for the bang-up finish. I mean, what would have been the point?

At home after supper that evening, I mapped out a private little schedule to while away the time on my hands. I'd spend one hour cracking the schoolbooks. The next hour and a half maybe watching a TV movie. And then . . . and then I figured I might just as well go off to bed.

And I might have, too. Except that just then the telephone rang.

TEN

"Don," my mother echoed. "Don who?"

"Petrie," I said. "He says you might know his mother; they live halfway down Woodward Avenue in the big green house with the shutters. Tall, skinny, brown hair, used to go with Mary Alice."

"Oh, *that* Don."

"He wanted me to go to the beach with him Saturday afternoon, and I said —"

"Beach?" My mother frowned. "In that skimpy, two-hanky swimsuit of yours?"

"And I said, 'No way. Beach is out.' So he said, 'How about the tennis courts downtown?' And I said —"

"Tennis? Oh . . . *well.*" Her frown disappeared.

"And I said, 'I suppose. If it's okay with my mother.' "

Mom looked pleased. It had to be a first. Me, actually deferring to her approval. What I'd *really* said to Don was, "I'll check it out with my social secretary, ha-ha, and let you know." Adding to myself, *It takes a guy to know a guy. I'll check him out with Jeremy and get the lowdown.*

It wasn't until noon the next day that I got my chance.

Jeremy was in a good mood. He didn't even mind that I'd lifted the lion's share of the tuna salad, leaving him mostly rye bread and lettuce. He was especially wound up about the new kid on the team. "What an *arm*," he raved. "Did you see Al make that throw from deep center in the second inning?"

Well, yeah, I had. But must we dwell on it?

"I tell you, every single Gopher performed like clockwork. Bob was sharp as a tack. And Joey, wow, what a powerhouse behind the bat! I can't remember when I've seen him play like that." Et cetera, et cetera.

Until we got to the molded gelatin with the whipped topping, where I got mine in. "Jeremy," I said, picking the maraschino cherry free of the topping, "there's something I'd like to ask you. It's, like, advice. About a certain, uh, person."

Jeremy sat up straight and peered over at me. "Person? Who's the person?"

"Well, I got a phone call last night. From this guy you and I both know. And I was wondering what you thought about —"

"Make believe you're not looking, Red," Jeremy interrupted with a croak. He had slumped low in his chair, his face suddenly scarlet. "Pretend you haven't noticed her. You're talking to me, see? That's right, keep on talking. Say *any*thing, it doesn't matter what. And when she walks by us, let me know. . . . Did she look over at me?"

"Well. It is a little difficult to tell, when I'm supposed to keep talking to you at the same time I'm not supposed to be looking—" I stopped. "Who is it I'm not supposed to be looking at?"

Jeremy jabbed a thumb over his left shoulder. "*Her!*"

Holly, who else? Dainty little Holly Longworth with the hundred brush-stroked blond hair that reached almost to her skimpy waist, the perfect-plus complexion, the "freshly manicured, well-groomed" look my mother kept bugging *me* about. You'd never catch Holly Longworth slouching around in jeans punched out at the knees, or a sweat shirt with the sleeves cut off at the elbows. She was moving our way, all right. And as you might expect, Holly didn't just walk, she *undulated*. I hear it really catches the eye. The male eye, that is. It didn't do much for mine. Of course, I'd been operating from the corner of one squinted eye while keeping my neck straight ahead. Not exactly the world's easiest position to hold.

"Well?" Jeremy rasped.

"I'd say she was looking . . . yes, she's definitely staring in your direction. And I think . . . yes, she is. She's smiling."

Jeremy groaned and scrunched lower in his chair.

"In fact, I do believe she's coming over here. Would it help, Jeremy, if I discreetly left? I mean, took my gelatin and—oh, *hi*, Holly!"

Well, nobody can say I don't know how to quit a scene as gracefully as possible, especially when faced with aloneness at a table elsewhere.

It caused me to wonder if I'd been so bright, limiting my best friendship to Jeremy Barnes. Furthermore, my mood was in no way elevated by the appearance of Mary Alice, dog-heeled by Bob Murray, gliding past me in the cafeteria. Neither of them glanced my way. Which was just fine. I had no intention of communicating with those two.

I finished my gelatin in total separateness. Watching, sort of, what was going on over at Jeremy's table. Holly, leaning forward, her gorgeous hair streaming behind her like bleached sunlight, was doing most of the talking. Jeremy just sat there with this slightly bombed expression on his round face. I think he wore a grin in there somewhere. It was hard to tell. I mean, it could have been rigor mortis.

In just such dim-witted moods of the moment are decisions sometimes made. I took it on myself to trash the consultation approach and rely on my own sound judgment. I would take Don Petrie up on his get-together offer.

"I know I suggested tennis, but frankly," Don said, glancing over his shoulder, "I had something else in mind." If he was checking out my mother, she'd taken off for next door. And why was I suddenly yearning for her to rush home? "My old man gave me the keys to the car, and it's full up with gas, so I thought—"

"Where?" I asked, not wanting to appear as

unnerved as I was feeling. (Don Petrie and me, together, alone, in a moving vehicle?)

He eyed me. "Oh, maybe to my Uncle Joe's dairy farm. It's only thirty miles out. I drop in there now and then."

Well, a *farm.* I almost laughed out loud. What a relief! I mean, what could possibly go wrong on a *dairy* farm, for heaven's sake?

How was I supposed to know that the "dairy farm" was, in reality, this duded-up milk bar called "Uncle Joe's Dairy Farm," specializing in flavored frozen custards? Or that in the back of the place were these electronic arcade games, to which Don immediately attached himself, under the impression he possessed special skills in operating the controls?

After a while he glanced up from the cutthroat game of Pac-Man he was playing against the machine. "Ever try one of these, Jody?"

"Nope," I said, looking less than interested. This time I intended to play it cool. Just keep on putting away my Butterscotch Royale, while Don Petrie showed off by running up lopsided killings. No way could I be conned into competing. I'd sit by, watching, applauding, pretending to be dainty.

"Well, I *said* I was sorry, Don," I repeated for at least the sixth time. "If you hadn't insisted that I play."

We were again on the move. Don was keeping his gaze strictly on the road and his hands strictly on the steering wheel. His mouth had flattened to a straight line some five miles back.

"And I'm sorry the other guys laughed at you when I skunked you on that last game. I mean, anybody could see that if you'd been a little more alert and faster on the rebound you could have won."

"Will you kindly shut *up*?"

Well, there it was. I, a mere novice, had showed up Don before all those people. We'd started out with an audience of two. And somehow it had mushroomed to maybe fifteen characters standing around shouting advice, taking sides, booing, cheering.

Don turned the car radio to some music with a jumping beat, doubtless figuring to drown me out. He needn't have bothered. I'd already committed myself to a vow of total silence. Never again would I open my big mouth and — "Why are we stopping *here*?" I suddenly yelped.

"Here" was a strip of grassy turf off the beaten track. How had Don sneaked us onto that dinky little road without my noticing? Not that this should be a signal for pushing the panic button or anything.

What I did know was if Don Petrie even *tried* to kiss me, I'd slug him. For one thing, guys with mustaches automatically turn me off. Although that straggly lacework under Don's nose could scarcely qualify for mustache status. But still . . .

It all happened so quickly. I mean, he grabbed me and stuck his face close to mine, then put his mouth next to my mouth. I opened my eyes just as Don's right eye popped open and peeked at me. And then his mouth came down hard.

He pulled back, looking pretty satisfied with himself. "Well, there! How was *that*?" He grinned. "At least I'm an expert at *some*thing!"

How could I tell Don (who'd already had his ego humbled at the hands of Mary Alice) that his "expert" kiss had been a complete bust? All I'd felt in the way of emotion was the taste of disappointment that had risen in my throat.

Okay, so I let him think he'd accomplished something marvelous. And I didn't push him away when his arm slipped around my shoulder as we headed homeward. I thought of it as kindness. How could I know it had made his day? And what was I supposed to say when he dropped over to see me that evening, the next morning, the following evening, et cetera?

Suddenly Don Petrie and I had become an item. Which meant I was seeing him more and enjoying it less. I tried to convince myself that, in time, I'd get used to straggly mustaches.

I spent all of one long afternoon trying to explain my feelings of frustration to Jeremy. He listened patiently enough. But all I got for my pains was, "Kind? Are you kidding? You call that being *kind*?" Some help.

I will grant Jeremy wasn't his usual straight-thinking self. In his own way, he was really suffering. It's hard for me to believe, even now, how absolutely unsmart an otherwise bright guy like Jeremy could become when confronted with Love (or whatever). I mean, just mention Holly Longworth, and Jeremy, the smooth user of many words, the logical planner, the statistical wonder, would turn into a stumble-tongued, red-faced dummy.

Okay, so maybe the shoe was on the other foot. Maybe the time had come for me to hear *him* out.

I led Jeremy to our back lawn, sat him down, and propped him up against the birdbath pedestal. "Well?" I questioned. "What's so special about Holly?"

He thought for a minute. "She's beautiful," he came up with, then frowned. "I mean, bee-oo-tiful." He rubbed at one ear, as if trying to summon forth Aladdin's genie to lend him rapturous words. His eyes lit up. "She's . . ." His voice trailed off. He glanced around, bewildered by his own fumbling.

So much for exchanged confidences.

Luckily, Jeremy's romantic fogginess didn't seem to interfere with his managing of the Gophers. Mary Alice, who had recovered from the incident at the boardwalk and taken to coming over now and then to sing Bob Murray's praises, let me know exactly how great they were doing. At first I planned on giving her the deep freeze. But I guess I was so hungry to hear about the guys and their latest exploits, I forgot all about freezing and listened.

"Naturally, Bob is the best shortstop in the whole league," she announced, glowing with pride as if she, personally, had invented him. "But Dave Lansing's terribly effective on the mound, too. Not to mention Joey Michaels and his fantastic batting average."

"I thought you considered the Gophers a hopeless bunch of juveniles," I couldn't resist sticking in.

"Oh. Well. Sometimes circumstances alter opinions," she said, trying to look newly wise.

"Is that by any chance related to, 'It depends on whose ox is being gored'?" I said sweetly.

Silence. Then, "Anyway," Mary Alice said, "the team's coming along just fine. Although I must say I don't understand your hands-off attitude at all, Jody. After the years of loyalty those really great guys have shown you, you've erased them from your memory as if they never existed. Even you should admit that's pretty childish. I mean, just because Bob and I —"

"Hold it!" A few minutes of Mary Alice Martinson was enough to test the temper of a *saint*. Which I wasn't. But I had to get it straight once and for all, if it killed me. "About Bob Murray," I said. "I'll tell you this flat out. That boy means absolutely *nothing* to me." True, oh, how true! I couldn't for the life of me understand why I'd thought his looks were so special. I mean, that nose *alone*. Ick.

"Then it has to be Jeremy," she pursued, brightening. "You resent Holly Longworth hanging around him, right? She's taken your place in his affections, and you can't stand being shoved into the background."

Patience, patience.

"But, listen, Jody, that can be taken care of. If you're really sold on getting Jeremy back, I'll get right to work on it and arrange everything."

"Mary Alice!" I took a breath. "Maybe you haven't heard, since you've been so busy with

Bob and all those Gophers, but I also have a little something going. With Don Petrie."

"Don?" Mary Alice let loose a little shriek. "And *you*? Oh, you have got to be kidding!"

"Well, I hadn't planned on sending you into fits over it, but — yes, there's something between us."

"Listen, I could tell you tales about that boy . . ." She caught my eye. "But don't worry, I won't. I'm just putting you on, Jody. Don's really tops. I know he's still sore at me for letting him down, and I'm sorry about that. But as long as somebody had to be around to pick up the pieces"— she smiled, this little facial crinkle, meant to show she was all heart —"I'm glad it was you."

So Mary Alice was glad. Why wasn't I?

By then we'd made it to the last week of school. A whole long summer of Don and me loomed ahead. Don had told my father he was going to stick around town for the summer. To keep an eye on things, he'd added, winking at me. Was it merely coincidence that I immediately found myself thumbing through the newspaper classifieds, checking out summer camps at the other end of the state?

"Summer camp?" my mother repeated. "Don't be silly, Jody! What with Mike's graduation next week and the advance payment on his first semester at City College, we couldn't finance a weekend on our back lawn. Besides," she said, smiling impishly, "that would remove you from dear Don. And you wouldn't want that, now, would you?"

Wanna bet? I said to myself. And dropped the subject.

My mother was part of the problem. Not only did she like Don, she liked his family. Especially after she discovered that she and Don's mother had attended the same high school at the same time, and that Don's father had been a boyhood pal of her favorite brother who'd died years before. Still, I really can't blame Mom for my growing panic. But why did I feel as if I'd accidentally stepped into a trap and there was no escape hatch in sight?

It mostly centered around the kissing thing. I mean, *Don's* idea of kissing.

The last time he had tried it, we were in "Uncle Joe's Dairy Farm" parking lot (after the other customers had gone), and I got real shook and backed hurriedly away from him, saying loudly, "No!"

Why don't guys ever believe girls really mean no? All Don did was move in closer and say, "Oh, I know how your mind works. Maybe means yes, and no means probably. That's how Mary Alice used to operate."

How could I explain to him that Mary Alice and I "operated" on different wavelengths? But Don wasn't in a listening mood. So I gave him a shove, pushed him clear to the other side of the steering wheel. And Don laughed, ha-ha-ha, and said, "Playtime, huh?" and moved my way again.

Ha-ha-ha. I wasn't kidding. After five minutes or so of my blistering spiel, he started up the car and dropped me at home.

But the dumb part was, he came back the next day. And the next. I mean, after all those *horrible* things I said to him?

Guys! Who can understand them?

The day after Mike's graduation, my life story took a forty-five degree turn. But let me back-track. . . .

There had been a party the day before graduation. And a party after the party. "A drinking contest," was how Mary Alice described it. Three senior boys wound up blotto and were hauled into the village police station to sober up. And Mike (who prides himself on keeping his cool) had staggered home around three A.M., looking pretty much out of it. The graduation itself was like one massive hangover, with "Pomp and Circumstance" clanging in the background. My mother called it a total disgrace. I guess she had a point. At least it gave the whole town something to chew on for weeks after.

So okay. That brings us up to the point where I came in. And Jeremy came in and went out. And Don Petrie came in. And went out.

It started with Jeremy and me. He'd wandered over that evening for the first time in days. And we'd sat around batting the breeze, almost like old times. I was feeling very relaxed. Glad to listen. Anxious to hear the details of the latest Gopher game. Not so anxious to hear that much about Holly Longworth. But sometimes you have to take the so-so with the good.

We were in the kitchen, working our way through boiled ham slices on pumpernickel, washing it all down with the contents of a

64-ounce bottle of cola. And we were talking about Holly. Again. At least he'd made it past the "she's beautiful" stage. I was now getting stuff about her "innate serenity" and "natural dignity." And more, much more.

Aw, come off it, Jeremy, I could have said. *Climb back down to earth with the rest of us. Holly's not that special.* But I'd seen his face as he spoke. The look of reverence. As if he'd entered a realm beyond mortal understanding. So I just took another nip of pumpernickel and kept on listening.

Our pleasant moment together was cut short by the arrival of Don, who just happened by after my parents had left for the evening. He didn't look exactly ecstatic when he saw Jeremy. But as far as I was concerned, Jeremy had gotten there first.

Jeremy poured him a glass of cola, and we all sat around the kitchen table staring at each other and trying to think up small talk. And then Don spotted the other bottle.

Vodka, it turned out, hidden behind the refrigerator. The way I had it figured, Mike had stashed it there the night of the parties.

Don wiggled the quart bottle loose from its hiding place and set it next to the cola bottle. "Hey, you guys," he said, "did it ever occur to you that we could —"

"Forget it," Jeremy said.

Don glanced away from the vodka toward a spot on the ceiling. Then he stood up, yawned, and ambled in the direction of the living room.

Jeremy and I went back to putting away slices

of boiled ham. Until suddenly we heard for the living room, "Hey, Barnes, isn't that your girl coming up the street?"

Jeremy looked startled. "Holly? Oh, it couldn't be! She said she had a guitar lesson tonight. Are you sure?"

"Would I lie to you? Yup, there she goes, up your front walk. She's knocking on the door. Your mother's letting her in."

Jeremy pushed back his chair and started across the kitchen. "Guess that means I'd better head for home. Heck. I was *enjoying* . . ." Whatever Jeremy was enjoying, I was not going to find out, because he'd made it to our front door and was gone.

Don came back, grinning as if he'd scored a great coup. He sat across from me and dabbed some mustard onto some ham. "Uh, your mom and dad gone for the evening?"

"Oh, for another hour or two."

He made his sandwich, then eyed the cola bottle thoughtfully. "You know what we could really use here?" he said. "A radio or something. Music to munch by."

Well, why not? Mine was next to the sofa in the living room, if I recalled right. So I moseyed in, and sure enough.

Don was right. Music definitely added something. My mood was mellowing considerably by the time he poured us a round of cola.

And another. And another.

I have trouble remembering exactly what happened after that. I do recall moving my lips slowly, trying to form questions. Like, *Who'd have believed simple old cola could fuzzy up the head this way?* And, *How come I'm having such a terrible time focusing my eyes?* The words were back there somewhere. But they hadn't made it to my mouth.

"Jody?" Don's voice came through a fog a mile deep.

I remember trying to stand up. But my legs had dissolved under me like melted butter. And I couldn't feel a thing when I floated to the floor.

But I could hear Don's voice breaking through the fog, hollering, "Jody, stand up. *Please* try to stand up! Oh, no, she's out like a light! I can't get her to come to."

I was laughing, down there in my cocoon on the floor. Because I'd never before heard Don Petrie sound so scared.

"Hey!" Jeremy's voice came through sharp and clear. "Hey, Petrie, what the heck's going *on*, here?" Then, close to my face, "Red! What's the matter with you?" And then, to somebody up there, "What did you go and do to Red?" Extra sharp. As if little knives gleamed in his voice.

Don's gruff mumble.

Jeremy: "Vodka? In her cola?"

Louder mumble.

Jeremy: "Joke? You call this a *joke?*"

Don, clearing his throat (or was my head clearing?): "Well, look! I'm *sorry*. No harm intended."

Jeremy: "Now that *is* a joke." And then,

"Well? You just gonna stand there? Get over here and give me a hand!"

I opened my eyes as much as I could. Through the blur, I made out Jeremy on one side of me, Don on the other. Next thing, they were hauling me, dragging me like a side of beef, into the living room, setting me upright on the sofa.

Jeremy lightly slapped my face. "Come on, Red," he yelled in my ear. "Come on, come on, come on . . ."

Tears welled in my eyes. And suddenly I was bawling, wailing, sobbing—oh, it was *awful.* I mean I just could not *stop.*

"A crying jag," Don muttered. "Good gravy, what next?"

"What next" turned out to be the arrival of Mom and Dad.

Believe me, there were plenty of voices after that. Beginning with Dad barking, "Who did this to Jody?"

A small silence. And then Jeremy's, "Let's just say it wasn't me."

And Don's, "Well, uh . . ."

"But, why?" From Mom.

"I was just . . . kidding around."

"Kidding?" Dad shouted. "Young man, you certainly do have one warped sense of humor."

I wondered if I should tell them about the sudden changes that were coming over me. Like the massive headache that had started at the top of my head. And the buzzing, like a thousand bees, in my ears. And the lump that had risen in my stomach and was threatening to roar past my chest and explode in my throat.

"Hey, everybody," Jeremy said before I could open my mouth, bringing his face closer to mine, "she's getting *awful pale*."

"Jody does have a nervous stomach," my mother commented from the sidelines. "So we should be prepared."

I'm always amazed at the speed with which Jeremy can act, when he has to. Let's just say he ran to the kitchen for a pan and saved the day.

Then Mom helped this wobbly, much weaker me up the stairs. She even undressed me and put me to bed, just the way she used to when I was a little kid. I wanted to tell her how grateful I felt, but the words got jammed halfway there.

"You're going to feel even worse tomorrow morning," she said, stretching a cold washcloth across my forehead. "If you think you have a headache *now* . . ."

I groaned from the depths of my being.

"You know, I've been thinking," she said, laying a cool hand on my cheek. "You may have been right all along. You do need some vacation time away from home. I think what I'll do is contact your Aunt Sue in Maine, and see if she can stand a live-in for the summer."

I was in no mood to object.

ELEVEN

The less said about my vacation in Maine, the better. I mean, anything more than a month of nights in the upper story of a bunk bed over my ten-year-old cousin Irene has to be too much. I spent approximately six weeks sleeping, eating, teaching my little cousin Jerry how to swim, feeding twelve chickens, one calf, and six cats, and listening to beat-up 78 RPM records, post-World War II vintage, until they came out of my ears.

I think Aunt Sue and I broke even. By the middle of August, she was about as fed up with me as I was with cousin Irene. So one day I called my mother and said I wanted out.

But honesty compels me to admit my cousin Irene wasn't the main reason I wanted out. The day before I phoned home, I got this letter from Jeremy. A letter just gushing over with stuff about Holly. What they were doing, where they were going, how really great everything was. It is not usual for Jeremy to gush. In fact, I'd say when you hear Jeremy take off on a cloud like that, it's time to wonder. And when I got to the end of the letter and read, "And, boy, will I be glad to see you back in town," my inner antenna was picking up vibrations like mad. Something told me I'd better get on home. The quicker, the better.

At first glance it seemed nothing much had changed in the old hometown. Mike met me at the bus station, and as we sailed along in Dad's Chevy, I waved hello to the usual gang hanging around in front of the drugstore on Main, checked out who was bobbing and weaving on the downtown tennis courts, and counted noses on the Lassiter front lawn as we crunched into our driveway.

Nothing of interest was stirring over at the Barneses'. Victoria, looking sort of forlorn, sat by herself in the lawn swing, idling it back and forth. And Mrs. Barnes was on her knees at the front walk edge, fussing with the transplanted hedges. Not a sign of Jeremy.

Mike and I had barreled in around noon on a Monday, so Mom was the only parent home. She seemed quite pleased to see me, and she'd set out a nice little lunch. Stuff *I* like. She'd even used her porcelain plates instead of those flimsy paper jobs that leak halfway through a meal. Even better, she really listened while I rambled on about my experiences at Aunt Sue's.

But after a while, weary of the sound of my own voice, I broke in on myself with, "What's new?"

"If you mean with Don Petrie," Mike said, leaning back in his chair and eyeing me for reaction, "he's back to hanging around with Mary Alice. She gave old Bob the air a week after you left for Maine. And he's hanging out with some chick from out of town. I can't think of her name, but wait —"

"Totally immaterial," I cut him short. I waited for him to work his way through a slab of cheddar cheese, then asked as casually as I could, "What's Jeremy up to these days?"

Mike tasted his chocolate milk. "Jeremy? Oh, he keeps himself busy. Still works for Longworth a couple of mornings a week. Plugging harder than ever with the Gophers. I suppose you heard they're tied for first place. The crucial game's this afternoon. Most of Arbutus Street'll be there to watch. I may even honor them with *my* presence." He drained his milk glass. "You care to wander over with Gail and me?"

I figured on going to the game, all right, but not with Mike and Lover Girl.

I got there while the pitchers were still warming up. The Meadowland Falcons' southpaw looked like real trouble to me. A sharp-breaking curve, and beautiful control of his fastball. Even scarier, I caught sight of a couple of Falcons taking healthy practice cuts at the ball, sending it flying all over the place. Anyone with eyes could see that Dave Lansing would have his pitching chores laid out for him.

Just beyond the dugout, Bob Murray was limbering up his good right arm, trading throws with Joey Michaels. He still looked all class.

Fast, true snap of the ball, greased lightning on his feet, perfect timing. I don't think he saw me watching. Not that it mattered, anyway. Bob already had enough audience for ten shortstops.

Including this smallish, dark-haired girl with immense brown eyes, standing not far away, gazing up at him as if all heaven and earth revolved around this one mere mortal. She was a stranger to me. But when Bob stopped throwing long enough to wing her a tender smile, you could almost see the sparks fly between them. She had to be his out-of-town girl.

Love? Was that what they were feeling? You couldn't prove it by me.

All around me shone other evidence of this Love (or whatever). I was beginning to feel like the real alien in their midst. To my left, Mike and Gail were cozily operating in a world of their own. Behind the catcher's backstop, Don and Mary Alice sat knee to knee, holding hands. And if I cared to look, would I see Jeremy and his Holly?

I craned my neck, spotting Holly along the third base line, talking it up with the center fielder, Al Marks. I looked in the opposite direction and caught sight of Jeremy slouched on the dugout bench, hair falling over one mournful eye, hands sagging between his knees. As I watched, he straightened slowly and inched his gaze to third base, then shifted it away. He looked pale to me. And somehow thinner.

"Hey, *Jeremy*," I shouted, waving wildly, forcing him to see me.

Jeremy glanced up, and something drastic

happened to his face. A grin popped through. Then he stood up and loped my way. "Well, well, lookit who's back," he said, sounding tremendously relieved, as if he'd given up the idea I would show. "Couldn't stay away from the old gang after all, huh?" He grabbed my hands and pumped them up and down. Then, keeping his fingers tight on mine, he leaned in close and pitched his voice low. "Red, you'll never know how glad I am that you're here." He blinked his eyes and turned them quickly from mine.

Jeremy was in some kind of trouble. Vibes were oozing from every pore. But what kind of trouble? And how should I go about finding out?

With a little poking around, I might have figured it out. Except that just then the guy who was umping the game clattered over and hollered at Jeremy, "Hey, Barnes, let's get this show on the road!" And Jeremy came to life, bustling around like a mother hen, gathering the Gophers about him, rattling off instructions, then sending them packing to their field positions.

I needn't have worried about the quality of the Gophers' fielding. It was snap, snap, snap. Like well-oiled clockwork. And Dave Lansing's pitching was top form. The first inning saw the Falcons popfly to left field, line one to the shortstop, and fan the air for three straight strikes. Not only that, the Gophers' half of the inning brought pay dirt. Joey Michaels delivered a single, stole second, and came in with the run when Benny Armand belted a double. Things quieted down after that. Benny got tagged straying off the base, and the next two batters struck out. But we'd made the first dent. It could mean the difference.

Team luck seesawed. The Falcons let loose in the second inning, collecting two runs. Then the Gophers, sparked by a triple from Al Marks, made good use of their half of the third, scoring two runs, bringing the totals to: Gophers, three — Falcons, two. And, more important, the Gophers seemed to pick up strength and confidence with every good play.

Until the fourth inning.

It started out okay. And then the Falcon up at bat slammed a clean one through second and third, and Bob (who was playing him deep) hustled forward, colliding head-on with the Gopher second baseman.

Bob fell heavily, landing on his right shoulder. And he lay there, obviously fighting back tears, while most of us stood around making sympathy noises because we felt so extra. Luckily, old Doc Alford, who is semiretired and managed to come to the sandlot games when he could get away, had more on the ball. He did a running-finger exam along Bob's shoulder and announced, to everybody's relief, that there was no bone break, just plenty of batter and bruise.

Game-time hung in midair while Jeremy escorted Bob to the dugout bench, around which huddled most of the Gophers, holding a whispered conference. I moved in on it and listened with both ears flapping. And why not? On paper, I was still a Gopher. So I had every right to know what was ticking, didn't I? Anyway, I was standing by, trying not to miss much, when I heard Bob Murray's recommendation for his replacement.

"You want *Red*?" Jeremy's voice rose to a squeak.

"She's your best bet," Bob said, sticking to his guns. "In my opinion, your only logical choice."

Silence, while the Gophers exchanged glances with each other, and I dazedly consulted with myself. *Me?* I snickered. *Aw, come on, Murray, you must have a screw loose. I haven't worked out with the guys in weeks. And if ever a spot needs a workout, it's shortstop.*

All Gopher eyes had suddenly beamed in on me, with the big question glittering there: *Well, Red? Will you?*

Would I? I let the question roam around my brain and back out, unanswered.

Jeremy had to be the one to put it into words. "I'm asking you just this once, Red," he said (and he wasn't smiling at all; he meant business). "How about it? Will you, or will you not, fill in for Bob?"

Well, put *that way* . . .

TWELVE

You'd think the Falcons had never in their lives seen a girl on a sandlot team. They certainly did get vocal about it. Sexist name-calling should be passé, I say. But what could you expect from those primitives?

"Ignore them," Jeremy advised, handing me my ball glove, which Mike had generously stalked home and gotten for me (after I'd badgered him into it). "Just get out there and show 'em what a pro Gopher can do!"

So I grabbed up a baseball cap (which is all the uniform we Arbutus Street guys owned), slapped it on the back of my head, and trotted to the infield. The ump had allowed me five minutes to warm up and make myself at home out there. One second of which I squandered sneaking a peek at the dugout bench and watching Bob Murray getting extremely chummy with his out-of-town girl. Which proved, I guess, that his injuries weren't exactly killing him. Holly was on the other side of the field, hollering something or other toward center field. Jeremy was concentrating completely on my warm-up. I think. If he noticed Holly, he did a professional job of covering up the fact.

So okay. Zip in with the old cowhide. Zip, zip, zip, around the infield. Back, forth, stretch, run. I was amazed at how quickly I fell into the familiar rhythm of infield play. And relieved, having no desire to make a complete jerk of myself before those taunting, chauvinist Falcons.

What can I say about what happened the rest of the inning? That earlier infield hit had put a Falcon on first. Dave fanned the next player, for out number one. The next batter up beat out a bunt. Placing a Falcon on first and second bases.

And then the next Falcon at bat hit a line drive straight at me. And I moved, zoom, zoom, zoom. I pocketed the ball, wheeled, and clicked it over to third. Tag-out. Third base clicked the ball back to second. Tag-out. Clockwork double-play.

It's remarkable what an effective piece of motion study can do to shut up a bunch of loudmouths. The Falcon side of the sandlot was pretty silent. And when I walked off the field, heading for our dugout, two Falcons scooted out of my path, giving me plenty of room to maneuver. Respect, they call it. Was that what I'd really been looking for all the time?

Whatever the real reason, it didn't hurt my new-found respect one little bit to collect two hits and steal home for a run and make a tag-out, single-handed, for the final out of the final inning.

It should have been quite a feeling, right? I mean, who wouldn't appreciate hearing such uplifting praise from a benchful of guys I'd been trying to impress with my physical prowess for years? Even Bob Murray looked proud. As if he'd done it himself, by recommending me.

Benny Armand, minus his catcher's mask, squeezed out room for himself next to me on the bench. He grinned, obviously tickled with the way things had turned out. "Hey, Red," he said, giving me a companionable shove with his shoulder, "we really took those guys today, didn't we?"

"Sure did," I said, shoving back.

"And next season, when you're back to full-time playing —"

"Scratch that, Benny. Next season I won't be back." And that was the truth. Once in a while I'm smart enough to quit while I'm ahead.

"If that's the way you want it." Benny shrugged, accepting it. That's one thing I liked about him. Nobody had to shove reality down *his* gullet.

A few of the Gophers wandered off the bench and back onto the field, allowing Benny some leg room. But he moved only far enough away so he no longer had to squeeze. The grin had dissolved, to be replaced by a half-frown. And the glance he darted my way looked faintly troubled. As if words were crowding their way to his tongue, and he hadn't yet figured out how to phrase them.

So who was going anywhere? I'd wait him out.

"Red?" Benny made a steeple with his fingers and peered through it. "Tell me something. Have you noticed anything, uh, different about Jeremy?"

I stared over to where Jeremy was slumped on the grass. Alone. "Well, I've only been back a few hours."

"And already you see where it's at." His fingers unsteepled and cupped around his knees. "Right?"

From the corner of my eye I could see Holly and Al Marks talking nose to nose. At least she was rattling on by the minute, her pale hair jiggling a dance on her shoulders, her hands gesturing, and Al was listening.

I glanced again at Jeremy, who was plucking at blades of grass, ripping them up the middle, sprinkling the remains onto his sneakers. He looked . . . I don't know. Would "sad" be too heavy? He looked as if nothing in the world mattered to him. Not winning the big game, not being able to soak in all those glorious words all of Arbutus Street had heaped on him minutes before. "I'd say it has to do with Holly," I ventured.

"You're getting warm," Benny said.

"I bet she's given him the brush-off for Al Whatsisname."

"It's not that simple. Al's, like, after the fact. Holly really did dig Jeremy for a while. But he —"

"Jeremy didn't dig her? Aw, come *on*, Benny!" Jeremy stood up and wiped his hands on his jeans. He stared at his hands, then jammed them into his pockets. And he moved swiftly to the shadows of the trees bordering the sandlot.

"None of us is sure just what went wrong," Benny said. "One day, they were a real item. The next day — *kapoof!* And when I just mentioned Holly's name . . ." He shrugged. "So after he blew up at me and the other guys this one afternoon, we decided to shut up and let him suffer alone. Something definitely did happen, that's for sure. And it has Jeremy pretty unstrung. He's, like, confused. Yeah, that's the word. Definitely confused. If I could just figure out a way to help him." Benny caught my eye and hung onto it for an instant. Then, "Know what, Red? If anybody in this world could find out, it's *you.*"

So okay. I would. Simple as that.

Only not so simple after all. Because even as I got up and started the long march to the border of trees, Holly Longworth yanked back from Al Marks and headed across the sandlot, zipping right past me and, with blood in her eye, aiming for Jeremy.

I didn't *mean* to listen in — what am I saying? Of *course* I meant to listen in! And I'm glad I did. I'll always be glad I knew enough, for once, to play it right down the line for Jeremy, when it counted the most.

Still, one must use timing and discretion. So I moved on slipper-soft feet, standing just out of view, not stirring. And I caught a full whiff of Holly Longworth. Bee-oo-tiful Holly of the "innate serenity" and "natural dignity."

At the time, I didn't get what she was driving at when she lit into Jeremy. What was she actually accusing him of? "The least you could have done," she shouted, "was remember who you were talking to!" Whatever *that* meant.

"But —" Jeremy said.

"Furthermore," she stormed on, "if I get compared once more to you-know-who, I'll scream!"

"Hey, now, wait! I didn't —"

"Oh, maybe not in words. But since when are words necessary to let a person know where she stands? I am just not going to put up with it, Jeremy! Do you understand that?"

"Well, gee, I didn't mean to —"

"You didn't *mean* to. Tell me more! You know, there are boys in this town who think I'm perfect just the way I am. And for your information, Al Marks is one of them. *He* knows how to treat a girl. *He* listens!"

Huh! How could Al get the chance to do anything *but* listen? If this was how Holly'd been operating, when had she given the poor guy mouth room? *Tell her so, Jeremy*, I shouted inside my head. *Don't let her beat you down like that!*

But Jeremy just stared at her and said nothing.

"What? No comment from Jeremy of the many, many words?" And then, in this funny, flat voice she said, "So be it, Jeremy. So be it." And she turned and left. Without looking back.

Jeremy stood there watching her go. His right hand slid to his face, rubbed along the jawline, and dropped back down. He eased his spine against the trunk of a nearby tree and closed his eyes. Then after a while he opened them, backed off from the tree, and moved along. Carefully. As if a vital part of him was suffering and needed special attention to stay alive.

I watched Jeremy make his way past the grove of trees, take a left turn at the corner where the Gopher sandlot meets Arbutus, then plod silently down the street. And I did nothing.

Did I have a solid reason for letting Jeremy walk off, friendless and alone? Not one that I could put my finger on. Just this odd, tingly feeling that cautioned, *Wait.*

But odd, tingly feelings do wear thin. And the longer I waited, the more uneasy I got. Finally, after consulting with myself, I took off like a shot down Arbutus.

It seemed I'd waited too long. Jeremy was nowhere in sight.

THIRTEEN

"Well, no, he isn't," Mrs. Barnes said, standing just inside the front door and peering out at me through the screen. "But he was, until a few minutes ago. He sailed in here looking a little upset, went into the kitchen, got a loaf of bread out of the refrigerator, and—"

"—made sandwiches," I finished for her. "Mind if I come in, Mrs. Barnes?"

She opened the door and followed me into their kitchen, while I mentally inventoried what Jeremy had hauled out. He'd strewn evidence of sandwich-makings all over the table. A slightly wilted lettuce leaf. A bit of hard-boiled egg. A blob of peanut butter. Strawberry jelly, dripping off the red plastic tablecloth onto the linoleum tiles.

"And then Jeremy got out his father's thermos and an old knapsack that was hanging in the back pantry, and he—"

"—took off on his ten-speed."

"Oh? You saw him go?" And then, before I had a chance to dream up some half-truth, she added, "I hope he didn't go far. We're having his favorite, spaghetti with meatballs, for supper. But you know how Jeremy is when he gets on that ten-speed. Time whizzes right by him. In fact, you'd be doing me a large favor, Jody, if you would track that boy down and remind him that I expect a little promptness for a change."

I sped out of there on the heels of all sorts of promises to Mrs. Barnes. Which I could only hope I'd be able to deliver.

You think it was easy? Just getting away from my own house without a hassle was like pulling fingernails. For some dumb reason, certain people I'd known all my life suddenly considered me a celebrity or something. Jody Shepard, the girl who'd shown up all those male chauvinist Falcons. I eluded the whole silly business by sneaking out the backdoor and practically tiptoeing to the garage in search of my ten-speed. It had to be the world's biggest relief when I finally hit the trail out of town.

Funny how scary the ride along the highway leading to Our Place could be when traveled alone! In fact, as the meadows and goldenrod and foliage thinned out, and those familiar stretches of brush and gnarled pines took over, I found myself glancing hurriedly over my shoulder. I hadn't remembered how ominous the elephant-colored shale could look, as it jutted out over the road, casting giant shadows that seemed to reach out for me. And for a panicky instant I wanted to turn and flee. Anywhere, anyhow, so long as it would take me out of there.

But I swallowed past my suddenly dry throat and kept on going, choosing the left fork, same as before, then moving carefully along until I spied the riverbed.

And there he was. Jeremy. Huddled on a crumbling slab of weathered foundation bricks.

I moved closer and watched him dig into the knapsack and take out his supplies (I guess you could call them that): An extra-sized paper napkin, the thermos, two sloppily put together sandwiches, and a large packet of M & M's. He removed the wax paper from the peanut butter-and-jelly and set that soggy mess onto the napkin, then wiped his fingers on a section of the napkin. He uncovered the egg salad sandwich and did likewise, and tore off a corner of the M & M packet, reached in, took one, and popped it in his mouth.

"Jeremy?"

His hand came away from his mouth. There was this silence, during with Jeremy and I stared at each other. Then he said, "Which one do you want? The peanut butter or the egg?"

I shrugged. "Doesn't matter to me. Whichever one you don't want."

Jeremy inched over, and I sat down next to him. I watched him split both sandwiches (and the paper napkin) down the middle. He shoved my cut over to me, picked up his half of the egg salad, and bit a chunk out of it. I worked on my peanut butter-and-jelly. He poured some ginger ale into the thermos cup and handed it to me. I took a quick swig and handed it back. Jeremy finished off what was left. I turned down my share of the M & M's. For which he seemed grateful.

For a while he crunched without comment. Then he eyed me. "You filled in at shortstop just great, Red."

"Thanks," I said. I uncorked the thermos and poured me another swig of ginger ale, wiping my mouth on the tattered remains of my half of the napkin. "You didn't exactly fall on your face as manager. Agreed?"

"Well, yeah. Agreed." Looking slightly more relaxed, Jeremy reached for his half of the peanut butter sandwich.

"About Holly," I began.

His fingers came down hard, squishing jelly onto a chunk of brick. "Don't mention her," he growled.

"I have to, Jeremy," I said. "You must know that." I waited for a reaction. Nothing. "I was standing around, listening, when you and Holly were over by the trees. And I heard *everything*."

"Yeah?" Jeremy's jaws guillotined two-thirds of the sandwich. He chewed more or less in silence. Then, "Okay, so what do you know now that you didn't know before?"

I thought that one over. "Not much," I admitted. "Which is why I'm asking —"

"Ask the right questions," Jeremy muttered through the peanut butter, "and you'll get the right answers. Maybe."

Not much to count on there. Still, nothing ventured, nothing gained. "For instance," I said, "what did Holly mean by, 'The least you could have done was remember who you were talking to'?"

Jeremy concentrated on his chewing for a minute. Finally he said, "Oh, that. Well, I guess you could say I goofed a few times. I developed the bad habit of calling her by another girl's name. And she got a little hyper about it."

Understandable. And intriguing. I couldn't resist a gentle, "And the other girl's name?"

"Well . . ." Jeremy looked away quickly. "I kept calling Holly 'Red.' "

"And this offended her?" I laughed. "She certainly does offend easily. I mean, you and I —"

"Oh, I *tried* to explain. But Holly doesn't listen too well. Or maybe I don't explain too well."

"And what about comparing her to you-know-who. What did she mean by that?"

Jeremy corralled a bunch of M & M's and fed them into his mouth one by one, ignoring my question completely.

"But what really got to me," I rushed in, "was the way you let her jump all over you. Holly was putting you down right and left, Jeremy! Why didn't you deliver her one of your classic one-two punchlines? I mean, if anybody had it coming, she did."

"Why didn't I?" Jeremy crunched his napkin into a ball and pitched it into the knapsack. "Because Holly . . ." The rest of his message had disintegrated to a mumble.

I cupped my ear. "I didn't catch that. What did you say?"

Jeremy straightened slowly. "You want reasons?" He brushed the back of a hand across his mouth. "Okay, I'll give you a reason. I didn't tell Holly off because everything she said about me was strictly on target."

"Meaning?"

"Meaning," Jeremy said, "Holly Longworth's a great girl. Top-notch in a lot of important ways. And I like her just fine. But she has one failing that cuts her out, as far as being my girl goes."

"And that is?"

"And that is, Red, no matter how hard she tries"— Jeremy's liquid, brown eyes held mine —"she can't turn into you."

Silence. "Well! Well, I must say, that's a pretty dumb reason not to —" And then I shut up entirely. Because what he'd actually said had just dawned on me.

Jeremy jumped to his feet and began pacing back and forth, talking all the while. "Now I realize this doesn't strike the same chord with you, what with you considering me a 'brother figure' and all, but" — he paused, eyed me hopefully, then clasped his hands behind him and went back to pacing —"these things just happen, I guess. I'm, like, stuck with this whatever it is, which sort of spoils any feelings I might have for somebody like Holly. Not that I regret feeling this way about you, Red. But sometimes it does get to me. I mean, all my life I'll probably be hung up on a girl who really can't see me the way I see her. And no matter how I try —"

"Sit down, Jeremy," I said.

"— I'll always be standing around watching her fall for every other guy in town, while I —"

"Sit —"

"— supply the old brotherly shoulder to cry on when the latest big romance goes kaput. I ask you, Red, is that fair? Don't I deserve a better deal than —"

"— *down*, Jeremy," I said, grabbing for his leg as he passed by and hauling him down next to me.

Jeremy didn't resist. Very much, anyway. But he did look a little scared, as if he'd suddenly stepped into the deep end of the pool and was wondering if he'd panic and drown.

I closed in the gap between us. "Jeremy," I said, "remember that old saying, 'Put your mouth where your money is'?"

Okay, so that isn't the exact wording of the old saying. Who cares? The point is, it got Jeremy right where I wanted him to be. Kissing me.

"Where did you learn to do that so well, Jeremy?" I questioned, pulling back after a while and giving him the eye.

Jeremy's mouth turned upward in a little smile. "Wouldn't you like to know," he said.

Of course it had to be Holly. I mean, how many other girls had he been hanging out with while I was in Maine? But then, if it *was* Holly, that meant she and Jeremy had . . .

"Does it matter?" Jeremy plunked my head back on his shoulder. "What's past is past, let the dead bury the dead, and all that stuff. Agreed?"

I mumbled something that was supposed to sound like, "Agreed." But inside my head I was working furiously on how I'd worm the information from him. Still, I'd have to use discretion. So instead, I dropped the secret words "spaghetti with meatballs," waited for them to sink in, then followed Jeremy to our ten-speeds and back onto the county road.

And while his voice flowed behind him in the familiar old rhythms as we rode along, I was still working on the neatest way to approach an absorbing project.

Namely, the cultivation and complete understanding of Jeremy Barnes.